dirty little
SECRET

Copyright © 2021 by Rachael Brownell

Cover Design by Emily Wittig

Editing by There 4 U Editing

Formatting by Classic Interior Design

All rights reserved.

No part of this book may be reproduced in any form or by any electronic or mechanical means, including information storage and retrieval systems, without written permission from the author, except for the use of brief quotations in a book review.

For my biggest supporter.
The man who made me promise never to quit.
Who would sing to me on my birthday, no matter how old
I was getting.
I love you, daddy.

WELCOME TO LAKE STATE UNIVERSITY

I'm in love with this series and these characters and I hope you fall in love with them too. There are so many names and faces, I want to take a minute to introduce you to everyone before you get started. There will be an introduction like this in the beginning of each book for you to reference so if you get confused, you can refresh yourself with the twisted web this group of friends is caught up in.

First up, you have the Palmer family – Max, Willow, and Evie. With the loss of their father, all three Palmer kids are grieving and attempting to figure out how to move on with life when their biggest supporter is now gone. Max is the oldest of the three. He's just completed his junior year at LSU, lives in a loft with his best friend, Finn Graham, and is the new president of his fraternity, Kappa Omega Lambda. KOL isn't the glorious fraternity it was when his father attended, and Max makes it his mission to restore the reputation in honor of his father.

Willow is a year younger than Max, having finished her sophomore year. She lives in an apartment with her bestie, Kendall, and her favorite day of the week is Taco Tuesday. Her suitemates from freshman year – Alexis and Piper – indulge her love of tacos every week along with Kendall. She's in love with Finn and has been for most of her life. The youngest Palmer is Evie. She's finishing up her senior year in high school and will be joining her siblings at LSU in the fall.

Next... the Grahams. Finn, Declan, and Micah. All a year apart, Finn is going into his senior year, Declan, his junior year, and Micah, the baby, is going to be a sophomore at LSU. Finn is madly in love with Willow – had her once and lost her. He lives with her older, protective brother, and is ready to risk their lifelong friendship for one more chance with her. Declan and Micah live the bachelor life together, enjoying every second of not having to be responsible for anyone other than themselves.

Kendall and Kora Potter are twins and members of Zeta Sigma Rho, the most prestigious sorority at Lake State. Kendall, younger by only a few minutes, was held back by her parents, giving Kora the advantage to experience everything life has to offer first. So, while Kora is about to start her senior year at LSU, Kendall is only a junior. She's also loud and lacks a filter, unlike her sister. Kendall doesn't get along with Max, her roomies older brother, but everyone else seems to love her. Kora is off exploring the world for the summer while Kendall is working two jobs to save money for a new car. One that has a passenger-side mirror since hers is barely hanging on after a little parking lot mishap.

Alexis and Piper shared a dorm suite with Kendall and Willow during freshman year. They're both incredibly intelligent – Alexis is on a full-ride scholarship. Studying is in their DNA and you can find them in their shared dorm, books spread out, or in the library most days. Unless it's girl's night at K and Lo's apartment. They wouldn't miss that for anything. Plus, they need to do laundry at some point.

Brady has been friends with Max and Finn since high school and Julian met them freshman year. The four of them can usually be found around a poker table, playing for quarters. Max was able to talk Julian into rushing his fraternity, but he refused to live in the frat house, so he shares a downtown loft with Brady close to where he works as an intern chef. His first love has always been cooking. Brady is a quiet, reserved guy compared to his friends. He loves tattoos, rides a motorcycle, and tends to disappear in the middle of a party. No one knows where he goes.

Colton and Kane are Max's fraternity brothers. They're also best friends and as opposite as two people can get. Colt is loud and wild, with shaggy hair and a beard that needs to be trimmed, loves loud music, and plays in a band. Kane is big into computers, a techy that loves to design anything and everything. He always has on sunglasses, but no one knows why. They're both typical frat boys once you get a few drinks in them – loud, obnoxious, and over the top. Charming when they want to be.

You'll meet more friends as the series continues. Things will get tangled – sheets specifically – and secrets will unfold. You can't keep anything from this group of friends. They see, and hear, it all.

dirty little SECRET

He's my brother's best friend.
Which makes me off limits.
My brother made that clear to all his friends the summer I turned fourteen.
That didn't stop me from falling in love with him. From dreaming about sharing my future with him. From wondering what it would be like to be with him.
It didn't stop the heated looks he'd send me when no one was paying attention. Or how he always found a way to be near me, to touch me. To protect me.
For six years we were fought against the waves of desire but the current kept pushing us toward one another.
Then I had him.
We collided with hurricane force. Our connection… explosive. It felt right, being with him. With the first kiss, I gave him my heart. With the first touch, I gave him my

body. When I saw the love in his eyes, I handed over my soul.

I should have known it was too good to last, though. The next morning, he was gone, and my heart shattered. I left it on his bedroom floor as I did the walk of shame.

It's been nine months since I laid eyes on him. Yes, I've been avoiding this moment. But I can do this. I can fight my attraction for one night. Even if the moment I see him again, I know that night is going to come rushing back to me, along with the days and weeks of agony that followed.

Because he still owns every piece of me.

dirty little
SECRET

ONE

Willow

As soon as the elevator doors slide open, granting us entrance, you can feel the bass of the music. I can't make out what song it is, but the beat has me swaying my hips before I can stop myself. A clear sign I shouldn't be here. It's been too long since I've felt this carefree. The last time—

"That's what I'm talking about, Lo. Get your groove on," Kendall encourages.

She has no clue how bad of an idea it would be for me to *get my groove on*. I tried to talk my way out of coming tonight. This is the last place I want to be, but my best friend wasn't taking no for an answer. The semester is over. I've been using studying as an excuse to stay in all year. To avoid *his* parties. But I've run out of excuses, and Kendall's been begging and pleading with me for days to be my plus one.

Yes, this is an invitation only kind of party. Not that it makes me any less comfortable being here. I have a standing invitation courtesy of my brother, tonight's host.

Judging by the increasing volume of the music as the

elevator climbs the five flights to the top level of his building, he extended more invitations that usual.

This could work in my favor. With so many bodies in his loft, maybe I'll be able to avoid *him*. My brother's best friend, roommate, and the object of my every fantasy since I was fourteen years old, Finn Graham. The man is built like a brick house—tall and muscular, with perfect hair and plump lips that taste like mint. Dark chocolate brown eyes that always find mine, sending shots of adrenaline to my heart, and other places.

We spent one night together last summer. I remember every second of it, even after consuming half a bottle of Grey Goose. I can recall the way it felt when he kissed me. It was all consuming. Hot. Passionate. Almost erotic, yet at the same time, he was gentle ... the way our lips danced as if we were the only two people who knew the steps.

I traced every curve of his body with my lips that night. Stared into his eyes as he thrust into me the first time. Tugged his long, brown locks hard as I came unglued beneath him.

That night I was granted my one and only wish. The wish I made whenever I blew out candles or spotted a shooting star.

Finn.

He was finally in my arms. In my life. As more than my brother's best friend. As mine.

The next day, it was over. The only trace of our night together was the raw skin on the inside of my thighs from where his five o'clock shadow had rubbed as he teased me with his tongue for hours.

So, yeah, avoiding this party, any party my brother throws, is at the top of my list. Because there is no doubt in my mind Finn will be here. And I've managed to do just that for the last nine months. Until two hours ago. Three shots of tequila and I was letting Kendall dress me up like a Barbie doll. Tight leather pants, a red halter top, and smokey eyes that make my blues pop. My hair is in long, loose waves, cascading down the middle of my back. If I'm being honest, it felt good to have someone make me up after spending the week studying my ass off, wearing nothing but yoga pants, a messy bun, and oversized sweatshirts. By the time my buzz was wearing off, we were already in the Uber and on our way.

"I need another drink," I mumble to myself when Kendall bumps me with her hip.

She has no idea what she's done. Tonight is going to end one of two ways.

1. I'm going to get really drunk, make an ass out of myself while flirting with everyone who isn't Finn, and pass out on the bathroom floor.
2. I'm going to get really drunk, do something stupid like demand answers from Finn, and my brother is going to flip his shit.

No, he doesn't know what happened. No one does. I haven't told a soul, not even Kendall, my best friend and roommate.

Why?

I'm not ashamed of that night. Hell, I'd love nothing more than to scream what happened in the middle of

3

campus for all to hear. To claim Finn so girls would stop draping themselves all over him.

I can't, though. Max would kill him, then me.

Max made all his friends promise not to touch me a long time ago. When we were all younger, hitting puberty. The summer my boobs finally came in. I remember the afternoon like it was yesterday. Max, Finn, and Brady were all swimming in our pool. Being only sixteen months younger than Max had its advantages. I liked his friends; they didn't mind if I hung out with them occasionally. It was the beginning of summer vacation and my bestie at the time, Lucy, was on vacation with her family.

Instead of sulking inside or reading a book from my summer reading list, I decided to jump in the pool with the guys. My mom and I had just gone shopping for a new bathing suit. I'd chosen a cute, red two-piece with tiny white polka dots on it. I turned fourteen and my body had finally started to fill out. Instead of being a stick-thin, little girl, I was starting to get curves.

Needless to say, the moment I stepped into the backyard and called out to the guys, jaws dropped. I laughed at their reaction because it was Max's friends. Who cared, right?

Wrong.

Max cared. He freaked out, wrapped me up in a towel, and escorted me back inside. He was muttering to himself the entire time about his friends not touching me. That I need to cover my body.

Overprotective Max.

I barely realized what was happening because my eyes were locked with Finn's, and it was clear he liked what he saw. I noticed the changes in his body as well. He had put on some muscle, his shoulders seemed broader, and his jaw more defined.

"Aren't you proud of your brother?" Kendall asks, pulling me back to the present. I need to focus anyway.

Stay sharp.

Keep my head on a swivel to avoid being caught off guard. To evade Finn and his smoldering gaze.

"Your brother is going to be a kick-ass president. I'm so excited for him."

For as much as Kendall and Max don't get along, she respects his position with his fraternity. And she's right. He is going to be a great leader for those guys. That's why they elected him.

"Yeah, proud. I don't think becoming fraternity president warrants a rager though," I reply, my voice dripping with sarcasm.

"Of course it does. It's a huge honor."

I honestly don't get the full impact of it, but I also don't want to fight with Kendall. She's a legacy, having joined the same sorority as her mother and grandmother. That means something to her. Max is a legacy as well, having joined the same fraternity as our father.

Me?

I'm anti-Greek. Not that I think there's anything wrong with joining, it's just not for me. I like to keep my circle small, and I get along better with guys than I do girls. I can count on one hand how many girlfriends I have, including my little sister.

Am I happy Max was voted as their next president? Hell, yes. He's been talking about how much he wanted this for the past year. He has ideas on how to make the fraternity better, more philanthropic. To eliminate some of the harsher hazing he's seen over the years.

So, I'm here to celebrate with him. But that doesn't mean I want to be here. Because being here means seeing Finn, and as much as I also want that, I know it's going to hurt the moment I lay eyes on him. My heart is going to be ripped out of my chest the same way it was the morning I woke up and he was gone.

It still doesn't make sense to me. He wanted it as much as I did. I may have been tipsy, but I know what I saw in his eyes when he pulled me away from the party. I felt the heat in his stare as he locked his bedroom door. And when he touched me, I felt something else. Something more—

"Let's do this!" Kendall shouts over the music as the doors slide open directly into Max and Finn's loft.

There are people everywhere, shoulder to shoulder. It looks like he's invited everyone he knows from campus, which makes me roll my eyes because Kendall was clearly missing her invitation. Not that he doesn't like my roommate, he just thinks she's loud and her lack of a filter pisses him off. More so when he's drinking.

All things I love about her.

Leading the way through the crowd, in search of my brother or alcohol, whichever we find first, I keep Kendall's hand clasped in mine. Neither of us are tall enough to see over the crowd, my five-foot-three and her five-foot-four stature swallowed up by the large bodies around us.

I recognize almost all of them, tossing a head nod here

and there when my eyes connect. Most are part of Max's fraternity, a few I recognize from the baseball team.

As we finally step out of the throng of people and into the kitchen, I let out a sigh. The open concept of Max's loft is great for entertaining but that doesn't stop people from crowding together.

Case and point ... the kitchen is empty. Which happens to be where the alcohol is.

"Beer or punch?" I ask Kendall, sliding around the island.

She thinks it over, rubbing the heart tattoo on the inside of her wrist as I fill my red, plastic cup with punch. She stares at my cup for a second, and I immediately know what she wants. Handing it to her, she takes a sip, her eyes widening in surprise. It's probably stronger than either of us are used to knowing my brother.

If the drink calls for an ounce of booze, he'll give it two. Multiply that by a hundred to make a large batch and suddenly the punch packs a punch.

"Punch," Kendall hollers at me over the music, attempting to hand my cup back. Shaking my head, I fill a second cup and clink mine against hers. "To our last night at sophomores. May next year be even better than this year."

And here I thought this year would be better than last year.

Nope. I was wrong.

Next year can't get any worse, I think to myself as I spot Brady walking by.

"Hey! Where's Max?" I ask, placing my hand on his forearm. When he turns toward me, I notice his face pales.

"Willow. I'm so sorry," he replies, pulling me in for a hug.

"What? Where's Max?" I ask again, pushing against his chest but he doesn't budge. Something's not right. I can feel it. "Brady! What's going on? Where's my brother?"

This time he releases me when I attempt to step away. Looking up into his gray eyes, I see his unshed tears. When he points down the hall toward Max's room, I take off in a sprint. The door is closed, something that would normally make me pause, worried I might walk in on something I don't want to see, but not tonight. I burst through the door, and everyone's eyes whip in my direction.

Max is sitting on the edge of his bed, head bent, phone in his hand. I can't see his face, his golden-brown locks hanging down and blocking my view. What I do notice is the slump of his shoulders and how they shake slightly every few seconds.

My brother is crying. I can't remember the last time I saw him shed a tear.

"Willow," Finn says, drawing my attention to him. Our eyes meet before I can avoid it, his flaring to life for a brief moment then calming. What I see in his deep brown globes causes my knees to buckle.

Devastation. Sorrow. Pain.

My knees give out, but Finn catches me before I hit the ground, scooping me up in his arms and holding me close. I rest my head against his chest, my body going numb.

I vaguely hear Colton, Kane, and Julian mumble their

condolences to first Max and then Finn, clapping Finn on the shoulder before exiting the room. It's just the three of us now and my body is on high alert. Not only am I still in Finn's arms but something is wrong with my brother, and I seem to be the only person who isn't aware of what's going on.

I wiggle out of Finn's arms, and he sets me on my feet but doesn't release me. His hands fall to my hips, and he pulls me back against him chest. I try to step away, his touch too much to bear, but he only tightens his grip.

"Max." My voice is barely above a whisper.

When he lifts his eyes to mine, I intuitively know my world is about to fall apart. They're bloodshot and tears are still streaming down his face. He flicks his eyes to Finn's, and I feel Finn nod. Instantly, Max is standing in front of me.

"Lo, there's something I need to tell you."

Fuck! He's never this serious with me. He sounds like Dad right now when I'm in trouble or when he's lecturing all three of us—me, Max, and our little sister, Evie—about the importance of keeping good grades and being responsible.

I stare at his mouth as he says the words that shatter my world. I don't hear anything after that, the room spinning around me as I try to comprehend what's happening. My body feels weak, my legs heavy as I take a step toward his open arms, but I don't remember the feel of his embrace, blacking out before I reached him.

TWO

Finn

SHE'S A FUCKING VISION. IN HER SKINTIGHT LEATHER pants and high heels, accentuating her strong legs. Legs I want nothing more than to be wrapped around my waist as I thrust into her, making her scream my name. Over and over again. All night long.

It's been too damn long since I last laid eyes on Willow. My little tree. Small in stature but larger than life. The woman who stars in my dreams every night. In my bed. Beneath me. Smiling up at me like I'm her entire world.

And the reason I wake up every morning with a hard-on, take a cold shower to relieve the ache in my groin and my heart. Because she walked away from me. From us. Without a word. Then stayed away for the last nine months. I've caught glimpses of her on campus but always from a distance, and I've never had the balls to approach her and ask her the one question I want the answer to most.

Why?

Why did she leave that morning? Why did she cut off

all contact with me? Why has she avoided me at every turn?

My calls go straight to voicemail. Texts are read but unanswered.

However, right now I need to ignore the longing I've felt for her. Not that my dick is going to cooperate. I felt the strain against my zipper the second she walked in the room. All it took was one whiff of her intoxicating vanilla scent and he was on board, attempting to lead the charge.

The uncertainty I see in her eyes breaks my heart. I can't tell if she's happy to see me or upset that I'm standing in front of her. When her knees buckle, I close the distance between us quickly, scooping her up into my arms.

It feels so right. Holding her. But I shake the thought away, knowing that in only a few seconds, her world is going to come crashing down around her.

As soon as the guys leave, Willow pushes out of my arms, sliding down my body, but I don't let her get far. I rest my hands on her hips, the thin sliver of skin between her pants and shirt burning against my fingers. I'm not ready to let her go yet. I'd rather hold her while Max delivers the news. I want her to feel my love, to grab hold of it, and hang on tight. Let it ground her. For her to know she's not alone in this.

Max might be my best friend, he may question my motives, but at the end of the day, none of that matters because all I want is to help her through this. To be her rock. I can't save her from what's about to happen, but I can stand by her side and let her know she doesn't have to wander alone in the darkness.

"Max," she says, her voice pleading with him.

He doesn't move from where he's seated on the edge of his bed. The same place I found him twenty minutes ago after he disappeared. His eyes find mine, and I nod my head, letting him know I've got her. That I'm not going anywhere. Still, he moves to stand in front of Willow.

"Lo, there's something I need to tell you." As the words slip passed his lips, I feel Willow's body begin to tremble. Not in anticipation but in fear. "Dad was in an accident. There was a drunk driver and he ... he didn't make it."

Willow doesn't say anything right away, only stares at Max like she can't believe what she's hearing. When he finally pushes himself off his bed and opens his arms for her, she takes a tentative step toward him. I'm about to release her hips when I realize she's going down.

Max cradles her head in his lap as he sits on the floor, looking down at his sister. "This is going to destroy her."

A statement to the universe, not meant for anyone in particular, his voice is barely above a whisper.

"We'll get through this," I say, taking a seat next to my best friend as he gently caresses the cheek of the girl I love. His sister. The one woman who could drive a wedge between us. "You guys are not alone."

"Thanks, man. I appreciate it. I feel so numb. Like this isn't really happening, ya know? The last time I talked to him ..." His voice trails off, getting lost in his own head.

I don't need to know when the last time they talked was, or what they discussed. James Palmer was a loving father. His children knew how he felt about them. Everything he did was for them. From working his ass off for their college funds, to the cars he bought them when they turned sixteen, and the bank accounts he set up, so they didn't have to work while in college. More than anything, he made sure he was always there for them. Every sporting event or special occasion. Holidays. Birthdays.

James didn't miss anything. His family was his life. There isn't anything he wouldn't have done for them.

"Your dad loved you, Max. He loved Willow and Evie. Hell, he loved me, and I'm not sure I ever did anything to earn his love. Always remember that. This is going to be the hardest thing you'll ever have to deal with … losing your dad, your hero, but do not doubt how much he loved you. All he ever wanted was for you guys to be happy."

Max nods, staring down at Willow one last time before carefully slipping out from beneath her head. Once he's standing, he leans down, lifts her into his arms, and moves her to his bed.

"I'll send everyone home," I state, pushing off the floor and moving toward the door. I don't feel like partying anymore and I can't imagine Max does either. It's been a hell of an hour and the worst is still to come.

"Nah. No reason to kick everyone out. I need a drink, and they need to see that they elected the right person for the job. The frat will only be as strong as its leader, and with me as president we are going to dominate this fall. Kappa will be the premier fraternity. I'm going to resurrect it if it's the last thing I do. For my father. For his legacy and mine."

With one last glance at Willow, Max opens the door,

voices, and music filtering in. When I turn around to question his decision he's already gone, leaving me alone with Sleeping Beauty. Tempting me to pull her into my arms, to kiss her until she's awake again. However, the last thing I want right now is for her to wake up in her brother's bed, my lips against hers, and remember that her world just collapsed.

THREE

Willow

Five days ago, my biggest concerns were passing my exams and avoiding Finn. Today, as I sit in the front row of the church—Evie on my right, holding my mother's hand, Max on my left—listening to my dad's best friend, Christopher Graham, giving the eulogy, nothing seems to matter anymore.

My father's gone.

He'll never wrap me in a hug again and tell me everything's going to be okay.

I'll never hear his voice or listen as he reads the *Night Before Christmas* while we drink hot chocolate and open our stockings.

He won't be there when I walk down the aisle.

Or have my first child.

Because some idiot decided to drink and drive. A man my father had defended on those same charges less than a year ago. He'd gotten him off, sentenced to community service instead of two years behind bars.

Because the great James Palmer was one of the best defense attorneys around. He never lost. Fought for his clients even when he presumed they were guilty. He believed everyone deserved the opportunity to change and that couldn't happen if they were behind bars.

If you needed help getting out of trouble, he was the person you called.

He was the person I called. No matter what time it was, no matter how stupid my decisions had been leading up to needing to make the call. He never let me, or anyone else, down.

And ultimately it had cost him his life.

As Mr. Graham steps away from the podium, the room falling silent once again, and I focus on the closed casket sitting only a few feet away from us. That's what hurts the most. Not being able to see him one last time. Knowing that the damage to his face is so extensive that he's barely recognizable.

Soft music begins to play as Max releases my hand, stepping up to the casket and placing his hand on top of it. He's a pallbearer even though my mother tried to talk him out of it. Seeing his face, watching as she attempted to change his mind, I knew this was something he needed to do. For himself. For my father. His hero.

The patriarch of our family. He worked hard to provide for his family but still made sure he was always around when we needed him. There wasn't a baseball game or soccer tournament he missed. He taught me how to ride a bike. To swim. To drive.

A true family man.

So, what do we do now?

As the casket's carried away, my mother stands, taking my sister's hand and reaching for mine. I stare at her, taking in her black dress, stockings, and heels. She's the picture of a perfect widow. From the emptiness in her eyes to the slump of her shoulders.

My mother is broken.

We all are.

I know she needs to me right now, but I need time alone. Her hand falls to her side as she leads my sister down the center aisle.

Bowing my head and closing my eyes, I listen as our closest family and friends, my father's coworkers, and half our small community shuffles out of the church. When the room falls silent, I let out a deep breath and lift my head to the sky.

Why? I want to scream.

I've kept the tears at bay. Held it all in for the past one hundred twelve hours. I can feel myself breaking, but I'm afraid once I do, I'll never be able to put the pieces of my heart back together.

A door opens behind me, a small gust of wind blowing a curl in my face. The soft thud when it closes alerts me to his presence, but I don't bother to open my eyes. Goosebumps pebble my arms as he gets closer.

The pew creaks when he takes the seat next to me, threading his fingers between mine and giving my hand a slight squeeze. A surge of electricity hits my system. Opening my eyes, I tilt my head to look over at him, studying his face.

His hair's been freshly trimmed, brushing the tops of his ears. The five o'clock shadow that normally graces his strong jaw has been shaved clean, giving me a glimpse of the dimple in his chin. But it's his eyes that have my hands shaking.

They're filled with promise.

"I've got you," they say.

"I need you," mine reply.

"It's going to be okay."

But it's not. Nothing will ever be the same. I'm not ready to say good-bye. I never will be.

That doesn't stop the first tear from escaping. Or the sob that follows.

Finn pulls me into his lap, holding me close to his chest as I let it all out. We sit like that until his shirt is soaked from my tears, mascara staining my face, and my breathing has returned to normal. Neither of us speak. There's nothing that can be said that will change what's happened or ease the pain.

I pull out of his embrace and stand, tugging my skirt down. Finn mimics my action, wiping his palms down his black dress slacks. When he reaches for my hand, I stare at him for a brief moment before walking away without saying a word. Straight out the front doors to where what's left of my family is waiting for me.

Max is talking with the pastor when he notices me approach, his gaze sliding past me to the steps of the church. Looking over my shoulder, I realize why. Finn is only a few steps behind me. Glancing between us, Max glares at Finn before silently ushering me into the car. I expect him to follow, but instead he shuts the door, and I watch out the window as he approaches Finn.

His back is to me, but I can clearly see Finn's face. Whatever Max is saying to him stabs him in the chest. His grimace is enough confirmation, but when Max turns back toward the car, the irritation on his face confirms what has kept me away all this time.

Max will never approve of Finn. Not as more than my friend. Not that it was an option anyway.

"Do you want any food? Something to drink?" Kendall asks, absently rubbing her tattoo as she speaks. She's been doing it for the past ten minutes. I'm not even sure she realizes how often she touches it.

"No, thank you," I state. It's the third time she's asked me. I know she's only trying to help, to be supportive. She's a great friend, but all I want right now is to crawl in bed and close my eyes. I know sleep won't come but at least I'll be alone.

The wake is even more depressing than the funeral was. Our house is filled to the brim with people dressed in all black, eyes filled with sorrow. Sharing stories of my father, his name constantly assaulting my ears.

If I hear one more person give me their condolences or say, "I'm sorry," I'm going to lose my shit.

Sorry doesn't bring him back.

What are they even sorry for? That he died?

Yeah, me too. It sucks.

My favorite line though: "If there's anything I can do …"

What do they think they can do for me? Unless they either A. have a time machine I can use or B. know how to resurrect the dead, there's nothing I want other than for them to move along and leave me alone.

"I saw little cheesecakes in there. Want me to grab you one?"

"I think I'm going to get some fresh air," I tell Kendall as I push off the couch. She's hot on my heels, so I shoot her a look over my shoulder. *'Alone,'* it says. She stutters to a halt, forcing a smile as she wrings her hands in front of her.

Five minutes later, after being stopped by more people than I care to talk to, I finally reach the sliding glass doors leading to the backyard. Once I'm outside, I remove my heels, hurry past the pool, around the storage shed, and down the small hill leading to the edge of our property.

Voices from the house float on the breeze but I'm too far away to make out what they're saying. Taking a seat beneath the large oak Max pushed me out of when I was five, I toss my shoes across the lawn and rest my back against the trunk.

Whenever I needed to hear myself think, this was where I would come. When my best friend and I would fight, I'd come here to get perspective. I sat here and opened all my acceptance letter for college. I cried under this tree when my first real boyfriend broke up with me. The same boyfriend who I shared my first kiss with ... under this tree.

The day I realized I was in love with Finn, I sat here and cried for hours. Knowing that I would never be his. That Max would never let it happen. More importantly, that he didn't want me the way I wanted him.

Then, after the night we spent together, I came here and cried because I'd had him, if only for a short period of time.

That's the day I thought I realized what heart break felt like.

Until now. I was heartbroken over losing Finn but losing my father … that's an entirely different level of pain.

"You really like this tree, don't you?"

His voice is deep but smooth as silk. It causes a shiver to run up my spine.

"What do you want, Finn?" I ask, my voice flat and void of all emotions.

"Where do you want me to start?" His chuckle is out of character for him. He's always been a quiet man. Well-spoken when needed but never a jokester.

"I came out here to be alone."

"I don't think you should be alone right now, little tree."

Closing my eyes, I let out a sigh at the use of my nickname. He's the only one who calls me that, but he hasn't since we were in high school.

"Max is going to kill you," I state as I open my eyes, keeping them focused on the meadow in front of me. Maybe the mention of my brother will scare him off.

"Max is going to kill me one of these days when he realizes how long I've been lying to him. Might as well be now. At least it'll give him something to focus on besides the pain."

Chancing a glance in his direction, my eyes travel up his body, taking in his long legs, trim waist, and broad shoulders. He's wearing a black suit, black shirt, and cobalt blue tie. It stands out against the darkness of the rest of his appearance, drawing my attention.

"Nice tie." Flicking my eyes to him, I try to gauge his reaction.

"Thanks. It's my favorite."

"Not really appropriate for a funeral."

"Depends how you look at it," he retorts, motioning to the patch of grass beside me. "May I?"

"Will you go away if I say no?"

"Probably not." His eyes light up as a smirk slowly begins to spread across his face.

My lips betray me, quirking into a smile before I can stop them.

I love fighting with him. Bantering back and forth. The push and pull of our relationship. It's always felt natural.

"Knock yourself out."

Lowering himself to the ground and stretching his legs out in front of him, he nudges me with his shoulder. "I know everyone's been kissing your ass all day but that's not why I came out here, little tree. I know this sucks and it hurts. I won't sugarcoat it. That's not what you need."

For some reason, his brutal honest doesn't makes me feel any better, but it also doesn't make me feel worse.

"If you're so smart, what do I need then?" I ask, resting my head back against the uneven bark.

"You need to let it out. The anger. The fear. The grief. If you keep it bottled up, you'll eventually break down and it's not going to be pretty."

"You don't have to watch."

"Never said I was going to."

"Then go away so I can do what I came here to do."

"I've seen you cry before. You don't have to hide from me. I'll still think you're beautiful even if your cheeks are stained with tears." His soft voice causes my heart to skip a beat.

Closing my eyes so he can't see the way his words affect me, I take slow, deep, even breaths. When I don't feel him move away, I reach out and push his shoulder with more force than necessary. My hand slips, my eyes fly open, and my head lands dangerously close to his cock.

"That's not why I came here but if it'll make you feel better …" Finn says as he helps me back up, holding me by the shoulders while he stares into my eyes. "I'm here, Willow. Whenever you need me. I'm not going anywhere, no matter what your brother wants."

I can see the lust in his eyes. We're closer than we've been since that night. The night I felt my heart soar only to plummet to the ground the next day and shatter into a million pieces.

"Last time you promised me something similar you weren't there the next morning. I'll take my chances going this alone."

Lifting my chin in defiance, I put on a good front, but Finn knows me better than anyone else. He doesn't just look at me, he *sees* me. The real me. He catches the shiver that runs up my spine, the flick of my eyes to his lips, the way my body leans into his even as I try to push him away.

Then he's searching my eyes for permission. The second I nod my head, he pulls me into his lap and his lips crash against mine, triggering goosebumps to cover my exposed skin and my entire body to clench from the sensation. Moving to straddle him, I mold my body to his and allow myself to get lost in his touch.

Even if just for a minute.

To erase the pain of losing my father.

To replace it with the pain of losing Finn again when he walks away from me.

FOUR

Finn

All I want to do is hold her. To promise her that everything is going to be okay. For her to cry on my shoulder, to lean on me while she learns to navigate the road ahead. It's not going to be an easy journey.

When she didn't exit the church with the rest of her family, I knew she needed me. I also knew Max was going to be pissed but I didn't give two shits at that moment. Her heart was broken, and I wanted to be the one to pick up the pieces and help her put it back together. For my hands to be what mends it.

Her father would approve. We had many talks over the years, leading me to believe that if there ever came a time where I decided to act on how I felt about Willow, that I had his blessing.

Odd, I know.

I never told him how I felt about Willow, too scared to admit my feelings to myself let alone to her father. I always thought that would have been like signing my own death warrant, no matter how much he liked me. However, I wasn't the one who started the conversation. It was always James. A man that treated me like a son, who made sure I knew I had a place in his family.

And when I pulled Willow into my lap inside of the church as she broke down in tears, I prayed for guidance from the man that is no longer with us. For him to guide me to do the right thing. To show me how to heal her broken heart and to help her move on with her life. Because she is currently drowning in her sorrow.

When her tears dried up, I thought it was a small sign of hope. Until she stormed past me when I offered her my hand. And when I ran after her, exiting the church only a few steps behind her, that hope faded. My eyes locked with Max's, his heated in anger while mine screamed of my love for Willow.

I've never been exceptionally good at hiding how I feel about her. For a man of few words, I wear my heart on my sleeve where she's concerned. I can't keep my eyes off of her, even when I try. I'm always finding a way to be near her, sometimes gravitating in her direction without realizing it. And up until the end of last summer, it wasn't an issue. We were close, friends who shared naughty looks, but nothing more.

Then it happened. The night I finally gave in to my growing need and made my move. To my surprise, Willow didn't put up a fight. She didn't play coy. When our lips met, it was like fireworks going off on the Fourth of July. There was an instant spark that ignited something deep within my soul.

"What the hell did you say to her, man? She looks like she's been crying," Max growls at me as he comes to a stop in front of me on the steps. He tucked Willow in the car before stomping over here. I can't see her through the tinted windows, but I can feel her stare on me. She's watching. "Listen, I know you two are friends and I know you want to help, but I think maybe you should back off. She's a fucking wreck and so is Evie. Let me handle it. If I need help, you'll be the first person I call."

I can't help but feel like I've been slapped across the face. Max doesn't want my help. His best friend. The one person he's always turned to in his time of need. We've been through everything together and faced it all as a united front. If there was ever a time he needed me, it's right now. Because if the situation were reversed, he'd be the one I called. The one by my side.

Nodding, he stalks off, getting in the car with the rest of his family. Once they pull away from the curb, following the hearse to the cemetery, I let out a deep breath and go in search of my own family. Declan is leaning against my parents' SUV, arms crossed over his chest.

"She okay?" is all he asks as I motion for him to get inside. There's no way in hell I'm sitting in the middle. I'm the oldest. Fuck that. Plus, I need to get out first so I can help carry James' casket to the grave site.

"She will be. Eventually," I reply solemnly, staring out the window as the car moves forward.

I don't say another word to anyone the rest of the afternoon, tamping down my own grief as I watch them lower the casket into the ground. As I see Tammy, Max's mom, break down in tears. Not even when we're back at the Palmers' house where everyone gathers to mourn together. To remember the man with the perfect smile, positive attitude, and deep, thundering laugh.

Laying by the pool with my back to the party, I let a single tear fall as I stare up at the sky, silently promising James I'll watch over his family. Not just Willow, but Max, Evie, and Tammy, too. I'll take care of them the best I can. As if they were my own family. I'll get them through this. Remind them that his greatest joy in life was to see them smile.

When the scent of vanilla hits me, I sit up quickly, turning my head just in time to see Willow disappear around the pool shed, her heels dangling from her fingertips.

I know where she's headed. Her favorite place in the world. The tree she used to climb when she was little to prove she wasn't scared of anything. The place she goes when she needs to think. To be alone. But right now, alone is the last thing I want her to feel, so instead of letting her run away, I follow her.

She plops down in the grass, throws her shoes in a fit of rage—which makes me want to chuckle, but I hold it back—and rests her head against the trunk of the large oak.

I try to keep our conversation light as I stare down at her. I can tell she's not in the mood to talk, that she wants to be alone, but I need her as much as she needs me right now. She just doesn't realize it yet.

"Max is going to kill you," she says as if it's not scary as fuck.

Yeah, he is. So, I might as well go for broke and spend what little time I have before that happens with her.

Because that's all I want. To spend every waking moment with her in my arms, by my side. To see her smile and hear her laugh.

She quickly changes the topic, giving me a mild case of whiplash. First, to my tie. It's my favorite, the same color as her eyes. A deep, cobalt blue. Then, trying to push me away when I tell her exactly what she needs to hear ... the truth. Because I guarantee everyone's been sugarcoating this for her, treating her with kid gloves, and that's not going to help her in the long run. It'll only make her dwell on what's happened. The same way she did after her first real breakup until Max told her what a piece of shit he was.

Trying to be the brave, strong woman I know she is, she holds back her tears as silence descends between us. I could sit comfortably in a room with Willow without talking for hours. And as the thought crosses my mind, her head falls in my lap with more force than I'm prepared for. Seeing her reaction, I make a joke of it, but the damage is done. My dick has a mind of its own and it's straining toward Willow for companionship.

Ignoring the urge to pull her into my lap and kiss away her unshed tears, I give her a small piece of my heart, promising to be here for her, no matter how Max may feel about it. Am I aiming to lose my best friend? Hell no. But I also can't live without Willow in my life. The last nine months have been pure hell.

"Last time you promised me something similar you weren't there the next morning. I'll take my chances going this alone."

Ouch. That hurt. But her words don't match the desire in her eyes.

And when she leans into me, her eyes telling me everything I need to know, I do what I've been wanting to do for months. Since I had my first taste of the woman who owns my heart. I pull her into my lap and crash my mouth against hers. Owning her. Comforting her. Promising her everything with my actions instead of my words.

FIVE

Willow

It feels right, I won't deny that. Being in Finn's arms. I know I am safe. That he will protect me. Care for me.

Unfortunately, my brain refuses to shut off.

I should be focusing on the way my body is reacting to his. On how his lips feel against mine. The gentle yet demanding way he is kissing me.

All I can think about is the ache in my chest. The fault line that feels like it is growing by the second as he rolls me onto my back, covering my body with his.

That ache should have traveled south the second his palm flattens against my thigh before slipping beneath the hem of my dress.

Instead, I let out a hoarse cry against his lips. The dam breaks and tears freely stream down my face as he gently pulls away. Gazing down at me, he holds my cheeks in his large hands, his thumbs brushing away the dampness.

"Tell me what you need, Willow."

Willow. Not Lo, like most of my friends call me. Not little tree or LT like he usually addresses me.

Nope. He's using my full name. I'm surprised he didn't throw my middle name in just for shits and giggles. It would have been just as surprising because Finn is serious right now. He's treating me the way everyone else is, like a fragile piece of glass, when all I want is for things to go back to normal. For people to stop looking at me like I'm about to break and they're just waiting around for the show.

Newsflash! I'm already broken.

There's nothing left to see.

Show's over.

Rolling my eyes, I turn away from him and push myself off the ground. Without looking back, I stalk toward the house. Toward the chaos. The sadness. The crowd of people dressed in all black, dampening an already dark day with dark clothing.

He calls my name, but I don't turn around, my bare feet picking up the pace the closer I get to the back door. As soon as I cross the threshold, Max is there, an accusing gleam in his eye.

"Where were you?"

"Outside."

"Where?"

"Why is it any of your business?"

"You are my business."

"I don't need you to babysit me, Max. I can take care of myself. You're not my father."

The second the words slip past my lips I regret them. Max sucks in an audible breath, his eyes going wide. I've never spoken to him like this before. Hell, we get along better than most siblings. I can only remember a handful of fights we've had over the years, and they've generally been around his overprotective, big brother actions.

Like right now.

"I'm sorry, I didn't mean that," I quickly blurt out, averting my gaze to the floor. Staring at my chipped toenail polish gives me something to focus on rather than the bitchy words I just spewed at him for no reason. "I'm just angry and sad and I want to be alone."

Placing a hand on either one of my shoulders, Max clears his throat but doesn't speak. When I finally look up, I see why. His eyes are brimming with unshed tears. "I love you, Lo. I just want what's best for you."

"I know." Wrapping my arms around my brother, he pulls me close and squeezes tight. If we're going to get through this, we're going to need to lean on each other. "I didn't mean it. I do need you, more than you realize. I always will."

"I'm right here. I'm not going anywhere," he assures me before releasing me.

"I'm going to go lay down."

He nods as I step passed him, keeping my eyes focused straight ahead of me to avoid eye contact with our guests. Stopping in the kitchen, I wrap Evie in a hug, then my mom, causing both of them to start crying before I retreat to the sanctuary of my childhood bedroom. It hasn't changed since I moved out almost two years ago. Same pink bedding. Same collage of pictures above my desk. There's even still a poster of Taylor Swift on my wall.

Without changing, I pull back my covers and slip beneath them. Unplugging my phone from the charger on my nightstand, I shoot a quick text to Kendall, thanking for her coming today and letting her know I'll see her back at our apartment tomorrow. I'm aware I'm in no shape to drive, and right now, I need to be here.

This house is filled with memories. Of my dad. Of my family. Us around the table at dinnertime. Celebrating Max's baseball victories, me winning cheer competitions, Evie when she was crowned the National Spelling Bee winner. Mom and Dad's anniversaries. All our birthdays. Every holiday.

But my thoughts drift back to family game night more often than not. Every Wednesday. Mom would order pizza, Dad would pick the game, and the kids got to pick the music. We'd spend hours laughing and fighting. Monopoly was banned multiple times but kept making a reappearance. Life was our favorite. My dad liked to make sure he always had three kids in his car, and he found a way.

It's comforting being here, but I also know that feeling will fade with time. I want to soak it all in while I can. While the visions of my father throwing Evie in the pool are still fresh. Of Dad throwing the baseball with Max. Of him grilling out in the bitter cold this past winter because I wanted steak for my birthday.

That's the kind of dad he was. He sacrificed to make sure his family was happy.

I feel the bed dip just as his scent washes over me. Sandalwood and mint. A heady combination. I used to get excited any time the smell assaulted my senses. Then I went to college and realized those scents, although a unique combination to Finn, were also somewhat common. Anytime I smelled either of them, I'd lose my mind when I couldn't find him in the crowd.

Freshman year, the guy behind me in my history class chewed gum every day. The same kind you'll always find in Finn's pockets. Halfway through the semester I couldn't take it anymore. I was fully prepared to bitch him out, but when I turned around, I was floored. He was gorgeous, his features the exact opposite of Finn's. Where Finn has dark hair and eyes that stand out against his soft beige complexion, this guy was a poster boy for California. White/blond hair, light blue eyes, and bronze skin.

When he caught me staring at him, he smiled, his perfect white teeth sparkling in the florescent lighting, the gum in question trapped between his two front teeth. He asked me out for coffee after class that day. I declined, and even though he didn't appear heartbroken, he never returned to his seat behind me that semester.

"What are you doing here?" I ask as Finn lays his hand over my waist, pulling my body against his. The comforter bunches up between his chest and my back, making me realize he didn't crawl under the covers with me.

"I brought back your shoes."

Shoes? Oh yeah, the ones I threw in the backyard.

"Thank you." Silence descends between us. My room is dark, the sun having set while I was sleeping. I hadn't intended on taking a nap, but my body was exhausted and had other ideas. I vaguely remember my mom coming in to check on me, and then Max.

Max.

Where is he? He'll be livid is he finds Finn in here

with me. I don't have the strength to fight him right now, or even to lie to him.

As if reading my mind, Finn informs me that Max ran to the store for my mom. He'll be back soon, there's no doubt in my mind.

"Why are you still here? I figured you'd head back to the city today, or at least to your parents' house."

"I just finished helping clean up. My parents left a few minutes ago. I wanted to check on you before I headed out."

"Thanks," I whisper, curling my hands under my pillow and scooting away from him.

"Uh huh." That's all he says as I feel him push off the bed.

Closing my eyes, I listen as his footfalls get closer on the hardwood floor. When I don't hear my door close behind him, I open my eyes to find Finn kneeling on the floor in front of me.

"What are you doing?"

"I'm making sure you're okay. I'm taking care of you the only way I can right now."

"And how is that?"

"By showing you you're not alone," he says, cupping my cheeks in his large hands and lowering his lips to mine in a gentle kiss, his lips featherlight over mine. "By showing you I care." Another brush of his lips against mine, and my eyes fall closed as sensation after sensation washes over me from the weight of his words. "By claiming you as mine."

This time his lips press firmly against mine, his tongue tracing the seam, begging for entrance. Kissing Finn is like basking in the sun. It warms me from the inside out, brings a smile to my face, and I pray it never ends. I could live the rest of my life happily if Finn kissed me every day.

Too bad that'll never happen.

"Stop overthinking it," he mumbles against my lips, angling his head, intensifying our kiss.

How he knows what I'm thinking about confuses me until I realize the deep V between my eyebrows is furrowed in concentration. Pulling back, I open my eyes and find Finn's dark eyes filled with lust, his lips pink and swollen from our kiss. On instinct, I reach up and place my fingers over my mouth, feeling my lips. They're puffy as well.

I wonder if they were puffy earlier. Was that why Max looked at me the way he did? Was that why he questioned me? Does he already know what's going on?

"I'm not letting you walk away from me this time," Finn says as he pushes himself off the ground, standing to his full height. His six-foot-two frame towers over me. Rolling to my back so I look up at him without straining my neck, I feel the determination in his stare even though I can't see his eyes from this far away in the dark.

"You walked away from me if I remember correctly," I point out.

"You ran away from me, LT. I went out to grab us breakfast, and when I came back you weren't in my bed anymore. You refused to answer my calls and texts. You've been avoiding me ever since. Not to mention your brother was irate that morning that I let you leave. I promised him I'd protect you the night before when he slipped in his room with that girl."

What girl? I don't remember him dating anyone at the time.

"He made us all promise never to touch you when we were kids," Finn continues. "I promised myself I would keep that promise to him. He's my best friend. But that night, I couldn't do it anymore. All it took was one look from you and I knew what I wanted. What you wanted. Max wasn't even a consideration in that moment. But he questioned me for days about what happened."

Oh. My. God.

Max knows what happened between us. Or at least he thinks he knows. And he's never said anything to me. Never brought it up. Hell, he didn't even fight with me when I'd make up lame excuses about why I couldn't come to his parties. He knew why I didn't want to be at his apartment. He knew I was avoiding Finn.

"I can't hide the way I feel about you anymore," he continues, his voice deepening as he takes a more serious tone. "I don't want to. And today he made me make him a new promise. To leave you alone and let him take care of you. To let you heal."

"Is this what you want?"

"No, and I won't be able to. You're what I want. Today. Tomorrow. Forever. I've wanted you since you wore that little, red bikini. Back then my hormones were in charge but not anymore. Now I let my heart run the show and it wants you, Willow. Only you."

Staring up at Finn in disbelief, I let out a strangled sigh.

Isn't this what I've always wanted? What I've been dreaming of hearing him say to me all these years? But now that he has, I don't know what to do with the information. I don't know what to say.

Do I want to be with Finn?

There's no doubt in my mind.

However, I have bigger issues to deal with right now. More important things to focus on. My father just died. I'm an emotional wreck. I have no idea what I want out of life anymore. I feel like a ship without a rudder, aimlessly drifting in the middle of the ocean, praying for land.

Finn could be my compass.

He could help guide me to shore.

And he would if I let him, but this is something I need to do alone.

I have to learn to be strong, to stand on my own two feet, and survive without relying on others. Not Max. Or my mother. And not Finn. Hopefully, he'll understand.

SIX

Willow

"Wait, back up," Kendall says as she pops the cork on a bottle of wine.

After having an incredibly quiet yet tense breakfast with my family, mostly because of the looks Max was shooting me from across the table, I hightailed it out of there. I knew Max was waiting to talk to me, to find out what was going on between me and Finn, but I'm not ready to have that conversation with him.

Not now. Maybe not ever. He's kept silent on the topic for nine months so he can wait a little longer.

Plus, I need to figure out what I want first. The two-hour drive back gave me time to think, but all I did was talk myself in circles. So, in true Willow fashion, I turn to my best friend.

"It's not that complicated, K."

"Yes, it kind of is. I don't understand. Finn wants you. You want Finn. Why aren't you together again?"

After pouring us each a glass filled to the brim and handing me one, Kendall let's out a sigh. Hopping up onto the counter across from me in our galley-style kitchen, her eyes bore into mine, searching for the truth. The facts I may have conveniently left out. Like how we slept together nine months ago. Or how we've been dancing around each other for years.

Things I've been trying not to think about since Finn's revelation.

It's no secret we've always been drawn to each other. Of all Max's friends, it's always been Finn that I enjoyed hanging out with the most. He'd come over and watch movies with me and Max when I was sick. Spent most of his summers in our pool. It was his shoulders I jumped on when we'd play chicken. He was the one standing next to Max when my boyfriends were threatened. The one that I called when I needed a ride home from a party and didn't want to get in trouble.

"Oh. My. God," Kendall exclaims, each word drawn out overdramatically. "You slept with him!"

So much for keeping some of the facts a secret from her. I should have known better. The moment I met Kendall I knew we were going to be fast friends. Best friends. We were paired up to be roommates our freshman year. We're both outgoing, but where Kendall is loud and lacks a filter, I'm quieter. She's good at reading people, whereas I try not to look too closely and mind my own business. It makes for a perfect dynamic most of the time.

Except when I want to keep things from her.

Looks like it was time to reveal the only secret I've ever kept from her. From everyone. I can't help but think it would have been easier to keep this from her if we were still living in the dorms. Or at least she would have been more subtle about her accusation.

Our suitemates last year, Alexis and Piper, are our polar opposites. They're both quiet, shy, and completely dedicated to their studies. Alexis is here on a full-ride scholarship. Piper just happens to be a damn genius and enjoys studying.

We pulled them out of their comfort zone when they needed it and they kept us grounded before we could have too much fun. When Kendall and I moved out of the dorms and into our own apartment at the end of the year, I was devastated they didn't want to come with us. I was going to miss Taco Tuesdays and Thirsty Thursdays. Study time on Sundays when they forced us out of bed at an ungodly hour on the weekends and we all went to breakfast together before hanging out in our shared living room and studying all day.

Unwilling to give up our new traditions, Kendall and I now host theme nights here at our apartment. And even though the semester is over, Alexis and Piper are on their way over right now, so if I'm going to keep the Finn thing quiet, I'm going to have to fill Kendall in before her creative mind runs away from her.

"Yes, once. But it's not what you think. And I don't really want to talk about it because it didn't exactly end the way I'd hoped it would. Plus, we need to table this for now since—"

"Did you not get off? Seriously? I'd assume he's packing. Tall, broad shoulders, big feet," she says dreamily, wiggling her eyebrows at me over her wine glass as she takes a sip. "The Graham brothers are every girl's wet dream."

"That's not what I meant," I state, suddenly feeling

like I need to defend Finn's manhood. Not that it needs defending. One glance and she'll know exactly how wrong she is.

"Look," she begins, her voice softening as she hops off the counter and moves to stand in front of me, "for what it's worth, I'm sorry it didn't work out the way you wanted, but I wish you would have told me. I would have kicked his ass for you or at least shot him dirty looks when I saw him on campus. But …"

Her voice trails off, and I know what's coming.

Sage advice.

Exactly what I was wanting when I first started talking to her, but now I'm not sure I can handle it.

Closing my eyes, I brace for whatever she's going to say next.

"I think you should listen to Finn. To what he said. I don't think he's the kind of guy that would say that just to get you in bed, especially if he's already climbed that mountain. You know him better than I do, you've known him most of your life. You have to decide if he's worth the risk, but I think you already have, and you're simply scared."

Before she can say more, I hear shuffling in the hallway outside followed by the door to our apartment closing. Opening my eyes, I watch Kendall nod once, letting me know she's going to drop the topic, for now at least, and she goes to greet the girls. Not having the courage to face them just yet, I hop down and walk to my room. Closing the door behind me, I let out the breath I was holding as tears well in my eyes.

"One," I tell myself. "Only one."

And that's all that falls. One lonely tear. I'm not even sure what I'm crying about. My dad? Finn?

Not that it matters. I'm done with the tears. For now, at least.

My friends are here, and I need this right now. Thirsty Thursday is one of my favorite traditions. I will not ruin it by crying in my wine glass unless the tears are from laughing too hard. Which has happened on more than one occasion. Generally, about the time we open the third bottle of wine.

My phone chimes in my pocket, alerting me to a text, as I'm about to reach for the door handle. Sliding my finger across the screen, I'm surprised to see a waiting message from Finn.

FINN: Just wanted you to know I'm thinking about you. I'm here if you need me.
ME: Thanks. Girls' night tonight. TTYL
FINN: <WINKY FACE EMOJI>

Pocketing my phone, I head out to meet my friends with a forced smile on my face. I don't even realize how big it is until Kendall raises her eyebrow at me in question as Alexis pulls me in for a hug. Piper's right behind her waiting to embrace me as soon as Alexis releases me.

"So, how are you really?" Alexis asks, holding me at arm's length, her eyes filled with sorrow.

"I'm okay. Thanks for asking."

"We were afraid you wouldn't want company yet. We don't want to intrude if you still need time," Piper adds as

Kendall hands each of them a stemless wine glass almost overflowing with the sweet white she opened for us.

"You know what, I think this is exactly what I need right now. Good wine and good friends."

Piper smiles at me, but it doesn't reach her eyes. I know where her mind is at right now. On her absentee father. She has a great relationship with her mom. The woman is a saint. Always so kind when she comes to visit, taking us out to lunch and doting on her daughter. She's proud of Piper, you can tell. Hell, who wouldn't be? Her IQ is one point below certified genius level, she's gorgeous, and she has the biggest heart of anyone I've ever met. She's never talked about her dad before and it's not a secret it's a touchy subject, so we don't push her.

There's a reason her and Alexis are best friends, though. They both have daddy issues, and despite them they're both successful and smart as hell. Alexis has to work harder for her grades, but she has the dedication and determination. Her family dynamic is the opposite of what I've experienced. Her dad is kind of an ass. Her real dad bailed on her mom when she was six years old. The man her mom remarried is an ass to her but takes good care of her two younger half-brothers. Treats them like royalty, spending the little money they have on whatever the boys want, while he treats her like the dirt on his work boots.

I've seen it firsthand, and if it hadn't been for Piper, Kendall and I would have given him a piece of our minds.

So, the dad situation in our little circle is a mash up. Kendall and I both grew up with loving, doting fathers whereas our friends never felt that kind of love. It makes my heart hurt more for them than for me. Because at least

I had my father's love for twenty years. That's more than they've ever had.

We spend the rest of the night talking about our plans for the summer, polishing off three bottles of wine, and laughing until we cried. No one mentioned my dad. Or asked why I started sobbing at one point, the wine allowing my mind to wander, my emotions sneaking up on me before I could push them down.

When their Uber arrived to pick them up just before midnight, Kendall walked them downstairs while I picked up the pizza boxes and empty wine glasses. My mind started to wander again, this time to thoughts of what Finn was up to. Where he was tonight. Who he was with. Was he drinking to forget like I was? Was he with my brother, helping him cope with the tragedy of losing our dad so suddenly?

Kendall slides up next to me as I'm filling the sink to wash dishes, causing me to jump, the wine glass in my hands slipping into the sink. It shatters on contact.

"Shit, K. You scared the crap out of me," I state, turning the water off and reaching in to pull the plug so I can clean up the shards.

"I called out your name," she replies, dragging the garbage can over to the sink so I can start throwing pieces in.

"I'm sorry. I'm not blaming you, I just— Fuck!"

Dropping the large chunk of glass into the trash, I stare at my finger, waiting to see how bad I've cut myself. It hurt like a bitch but there's still no blood. Giving my middle finger a little pinch, I instantly regret my decision when blood rushes to the surface, dripping down my hand.

"Damn. You got that pretty good. Let me get a bandage." Kendall rushes out of the kitchen while I hold my bleeding finger over the garbage can. I can hear her rummaging around in the cabinet, and then she's back in front of me, holding up the tiniest band-aid I've ever seen. "This is all we have."

"I'll just wrap some paper towel around it."

Ten minutes later, Kendall and I have managed to wrap my finger in three layers of paper towel, but it refuses to stop bleeding through the cheap cloth. Now I'm wishing we'd paid extra for the good stuff. This barely soaks up water. Why did I think it'd stop my finger from bleeding?

"We should probably take you to get it checked out. You might need stitches," she says, slipping her shoes on without waiting for me to agree to her demands. Per usual.

"Neither of us can drive, K," I point out. "Which is probably why I'm bleeding so much. Alcohol thins your blood."

She seems to think about our predicament for a second before asking for my phone. I hand it over without a second thought, watching as she feverishly taps against the screen.

"There," she says, sounding proud of herself. "Our ride will be here in ten minutes."

"I could have ordered us an Uber. You didn't have to do it for me."

"Oh, I didn't order us an Uber. I ordered you a knight in shining armor." The smirk on Kendall's face causes my stomach to drop as my phone chimes in my hand.

FINN: On my way. Hold your hand above your heart.

"I'm going to kill you," I mumble, not that Kendall is listening to me.

Nope. She kicks her shoes back off and saunters to her bedroom, closing the door behind her. Leaving me in Finn's capable hands. If I didn't know better, I'd think my best friend was trying to play matchmaker. Oh, wait ... I do know her, and that's exactly what she's doing.

SEVEN

Finn

I couldn't stop myself from seeing her one last time before I left. From checking on her. Kissing her. My heart was aching for just one more glance, one more touch. Because I can't protect her from what's happening right now, but I can help her heal.

Despite what Max thinks.

She needs me and I need her.

As soon as I heard Max's car pull out of the driveway, I darted up the stairs toward her room. Tammy watched me go with an amused smile on her face, the first genuine smile I'd see from her all day. She'd put up a good front during the wake, but her smile never reached her eyes, and I can't imagine it will anytime soon. She lost the love of her life, the father of her children, her husband of more than twenty years.

Watching Tammy is what made me realize how short life really is. We have today but tomorrow isn't guaranteed. Why am I waiting to tell Willow how I feel? What's the point in denying either of us a life of happiness together when we don't know how much longer we have left on this earth?

There isn't one.

That's why I laid my heart on the line with her. I told her everything I've wanted to say for years.

I love her. Always have. Always will.

I intend to marry this girl one day. To officially make her mine. To have kids and grow old together.

This isn't a new revelation. I've felt this way for years, but I've been too afraid of ruining our friendship to act. But what we have goes way beyond friendship.

The words *I love you* were on the tip of my tongue, but the expression on her face said she wasn't ready to hear them yet. I bared my soul to her. She was still in shock from losing her father, and what I added shook her world up even more. So, I bit my tongue and left her there to think about what I said before I couldn't stop myself from saying more.

And as I laid in bed last night, I replayed every moment I've spent with Willow since realizing I loved her. From summers in her parents' pool in high school to parties on campus. I can't remember a time I wasn't over the moon for her. That my heart didn't beat for hers. That I wouldn't have done anything to make her smile.

Which is what I'm contemplating telling Max right now as he stares me down, waiting for me to answer him.

"Just tell me the truth. Is there something going on between you and Willow?"

He's barely holding his anger in. His hands are fisted at his sides, and his eyes burning into mine. I want to tell him everything, lay it all out on the table. He's my best friend, LT's his sister. He deserves to know.

I hold back for two reasons.

1. I have no idea how Willow wants to handle this.
2. I don't honestly know what's going on between us yet. She needs time and I'm giving her that.

"It's not what you think, for starters." That might be a lie. I have no idea what he *thinks* is going on but still I maintain eye contact. I need him to see that I'm not backing down, that I'm willing to fight for her even if it means fighting him. "You know I love Lo, that I'll always protect her. She's hurting right now, and I just want to be there for her. She needs someone who's not going through the same heartache to lean on."

"That's why she has Kendall," he practically spits.

I want to laugh in his face. He can't stand that girl. For no other reason than she doesn't bite her tongue around him like most other people. And now he wants to use her as an excuse to keep me away from LT? Not gonna happen.

"And she has me. I know you don't like it; I know you told me to leave her alone, but I won't do it. I won't abandon her. And do you know why?"

"Enlighten me," he goads, his voice angrier than I've ever heard him.

"Because if the situation were reversed and something happened to my dad, you'd do the same for me. You'd help me even when I tried to push you away. You'd make sure my brothers were okay. My mom. Because we're family, man. You don't give up on family. You don't let them mourn alone."

He averts his eyes from mine, and I know I've finally gotten through to him. And what I said wasn't a lie, aside from omitting a few key details. Max's shoulders sag as he rests back against the leather couch in our loft. I can tell he's struggling but he isn't the kind of guy who wants to talk about his feelings. When he's ready, when he wants to get it off his chest, he'll come to me. Until then, I need to give him space to figure out what he feels.

"I can't watch her cry," he finally says as he stares at the ceiling. "It breaks me every time. Evie and my mom have been nothing but tears … but Willow, she's strong. So, when she cries it breaks me all over again. She's holding it together better than the rest of us."

"No, she's not. She's bottling it up."

"I won't stop you from being her shoulder to cry on, but if I find out it's more than that, that you're lying to me …"

I want to laugh but I can hear the anguish in his voice. He's broken and the last thing he needs right now is a reason to be even more pissed off at the world.

So, I'll keep this a secret from him until he can handle it. It'll be the first time in my life I haven't been completely honest with Max. In the end, I hope he sees that I can make her happy. That I'm good enough for her. That I'll protect her, always, and love her until I take my last breath.

Thinking about Willow, talking about her with Max, makes me miss her. So, I send her a text. She's having girls' night, which brings a smile to my face. She's keeping with her regular routine, trying to get back to some semblance of normalcy.

After showering off the long weekend, I'm about to crawl in bed when I get another text from her. My heart skips a beat until I read what it says, causing it to stop completely.

EIGHT

WILLOW

BY THE TIME FINN TUCKS ME IN THE PASSENGER SEAT OF his car, I am starting to feel woozy. My hand is pressed against my chest, over my heart as instructed, and wrapped in a kitchen towel already stained with blood.

My first thought when he arrives is, *Damn, he looks good.*

His hair's damp, as if he's just stepped out of the shower. His jeans hang low on his hips and his T-shirt is stretched tight across his chest. He looks drastically different than the last time I saw him. Though he looked good in a suit, this is my favorite look on Finn.

My second thought, *I'm going to ruin his car.*

Finn spent most of his teen years restoring a black 1970 Ford Mustang Mach 1 back to pristine condition. I remember nights he'd come over smelling like oil and grease, black soot still under his nails long after he showered. The last thing I wanted to do was get blood on the leather seats. This car was his baby.

"Deep breaths," Finn encourages as he pulls away

from the curb, accelerating as if I'm on the verge of dying at any second.

"Are you telling me or you?" I try to joke but he doesn't even crack a smile. "I'm fine, really. Kendall didn't need to call you. We could have taken an Uber."

"What did I tell you the other day, LT? I'll always be there for you."

"Yes, but that doesn't mean you needed to give up whatever plans you had tonight to drive me to the hospital. It's going to take hours, and I'm sure you'd rather be doing whatever it was you were doing."

I don't want to ask where he was or who he was with. I've been wondering about him all night, allowing my mind to slip away from the conversation with my friends from time to time. Daydreaming about our summers spent by the pool. Wondering if I screwed up my one chance with him the other night when I pushed him away.

I can't right now. I'm sorry.

I wanted to tell him I felt the same. That I wanted to be with him, too. More than anything. He was all I wanted. But I couldn't. So, I pushed him away and yet here he is, pushing back. Finding a way to be around me. In my life.

"There's nowhere else I'd rather be," he finally says as we pull into the parking lot of the emergency room.

That doesn't tell me what he was up to before Kendall text him which is what I really want to know.

I'm shown back to a room as soon as we arrive. One look at my finger by the triage nurse and I was whisked away. Finn wasn't allowed to come back with me, but that didn't stop him from staying updated about what was going on.

FINN: Has the doctor come in yet?
ME: No. I told you I'd let you know as soon as he does.
FINN: You've been back there for twenty minutes. How long did they say before he would be in?
ME: They didn't. STOP WORRYING.
FINN: I'll always worry about you, LT. Especially when I can't see for myself that you're okay.
ME: You saw me in the car. Didn't I look okay to you?
FINN: You looked gorgeous but that's not what I meant, and you know it. I should have lied and said you were my fiancée, so they'd let me back there.

His words cause a shiver to run up my spine. I stare at his message, reading it over and over again, wondering what it would be like if I really were Finn's fiancée. What would life be like with him? I can't even imagine it. Our *relationship* lasted all of twelve hours last time. Not long enough to make a proper assessment of whether or not he's boyfriend material let alone husband material.

FINN: Where did you go? Did the doctor come in finally?
ME: No. It's hard to type with one hand.
FINN: You weren't having an issue a minute ago. Where'd you go? I didn't mean to freak you out, LT. It's not like I'm about to drop to one knee, but I won't lie and say I've never thought about us together. Married. Kids. A house and a dog. The whole package.

Holy hell! I can't deal with this right now. I appreciate Finn's honesty but it's too much to deal with. I still haven't figured out where I want to go from here, and now he's putting ideas in my head. Ideas I'd love nothing more than to entertain. Me pregnant with Finn's child for starters.

ME: Doc's here.

It's a lie and I guarantee he knows it. Thankfully, he doesn't call me out, and five minutes later, the doctor really does arrive. Six stitches and an hour after the being called back to the room, Finn and I are walking out of the ER. He reaches for my good hand but hesitates when he sees the look in my eye.

The drive back to my apartment is tense silence. There's so much I want to say. Questions I'm dying to ask him, but I know I'm not ready. My grief is still all-consuming at times, and I know if I give him a chance and he lets me down, my heart will never recover.

Finn walks me up the two flights of stairs to my door. We stand in the hall staring at each other like two preteens unsure of how to say good-bye at the end of an awkward first date. Just as I'm about to thank him for helping me again, the door opens, and a very sleepy Kendall is standing on the other side.

"I thought I heard the rumble of Finn's badass skunk," Kendall says, motioning for us to come inside. It almost feels like she's inviting me into my own apartment.

"Skunk?" Finn inquires as he toes off his shoes, closing the door behind him.

Kendall and Finn haven't spent much time together. They've met in passing a handful of times, mostly at parties our freshman year before I began avoiding Finn like the plague. They don't have much in common but that never stopped Kendall from interacting with people like they're old friends.

"Yeah. That white racing strip reminds me of a skunk. Why? What do you call your car?"

"Sasha."

"Sasha? You actually named your car?" Kendall seems surprised by this. I'm not, of course. My brother named his first truck. It was a piece of shit, didn't like to start in the winter, and the gas gauge didn't work, but he loved that truck and said *she* deserved a name.

It must be a guy thing.

"She takes care of me, and I take care of her. She deserved a name," he explains, echoing my thoughts.

"Well, thank you and *Sasha* for taking such good care of my roomie tonight. Now, if you'll excuse me, I'm going back to bed. I have beauty sleep to catch up on."

She sashays away, her little sleep shorts accentuating her curves.

When I turn to Finn, I find him watching me intently. I get lost in the sea of emotions in his eyes. The magnetic pull I feel any time he's around wraps itself around me, and I'm suddenly standing right in front of him. His hands are on my waist and my good palm is flat against his chest, over his heart.

"Mind if I stay here tonight?" he asks. When I don't answer right away, he continues, giving my hips a little squeeze, "I'd feel better if I was here to change your bandage in the morning."

He could always come back, I want to point out. He only lives six blocks away on the other side of Lake State's downtown campus.

"Sure," I hear myself say. I must be having some sort of out-of-body experience right now from the blood loss.

Wrapping my hand around Finn's, I tug him down the hall toward my bedroom. The door closes behind us with a soft click, our eyes meeting over my shoulder. Without a second thought, I release his hand and turn toward him, pulling my T-shirt over my head and dropping it to the floor. He does the same, tossing his shirt on top of mine.

When I go to unbutton my jeans, I fumble, the large dressing the doctor put on my finger in the way. Finn's hands land on mine, pulling them away before returning to my button and slowly popping it through the eyehole. Sucking in a breath when his fingers skim my exposed skin, I hold it, waiting for him to pull away. Instead, he slowly lowers my zipper, the sound echoing in my ears, seeming to go on forever.

My stomach drops, my arousal heightened. My panties are damp, my nipples rubbing against the material of my bra.

Jesus. He hasn't even touched me really and I'm a hot mess.

"I think you better take it from here or I'm going to have to leave," Finn whispers, cutting through the silence.

Apparently, I'm not the only one effected by the sexual tension in the room.

Shimmying my jeans over my hips, I let them pool at

my feet and step out, kicking them onto our growing pile of clothes with my toe. I expect Finn to mimic my actions, but instead, he flicks the overhead light off, bathing us in darkness.

"What are you doing?" I ask as I blindly reach for my bed, pulling back my covers.

"Putting you to bed."

"Are you going to sleep in your jeans?"

He doesn't respond until after I've crawled under the covers. He slides in behind me, gently wrapping one arm over my waist and tucking me against his body.

Heaven.

"There has to be something between us, LT. Otherwise, neither of us will get any sleep. I want the next time we make love to be when we're both ready, and I know you're not right now."

Make love.

His choice of words doesn't escape me.

"Can I at least take my bra off?" I ask, not wanting to press the issue or make things awkward but knowing I won't be able to get comfortable if I leave it on.

Instead of granting me permission, I feel Finn's hand slide up my back. With expertise I didn't realize he possessed, he releases the clasp of my bra with one hand, on his first attempt. My last boyfriend refused to take my bra off, saying that they were made to test a man's patience.

He wasn't a man. Maybe that's why he couldn't get it, or me, off. Not even on his third try.

Finn gently pulls the material away from my chest,

carefully sliding it down my arms and over my injured hand before tossing it into the darkness.

"Better?" he asks.

"You tell me?" I joke.

Finn's body stiffens behind me, his arm that's now back around my waist tightening it's hold, pulling me closer.

I can feel the tent in his jeans against my ass. If I move at all, I'll be rubbing against him and the last thing I want to do is tease him. But I want to feel him against me. Without his jeans acting as a protective barrier. Skin on skin.

It's not like we haven't done this before.

Sure, I have no idea what I want right now but that doesn't mean I don't have needs. Needs he could satisfy and vice versa. We could be fuck buddies. I could protect myself from getting hurt by cutting off the emotional aspect of things. All it'd be is dirty, kinky, hot sex. All the time.

"Willow," he groans. That's when I realize I'm acting on my thoughts. My ass is rubbing against his cock, his hands tightening their hold on my hips.

Stopping, unsure of what to do next, I feel Finn scramble away from me. I'm about to ask where he's going when the bed dips again and my body is pulled tightly against his. He's completely naked, gripping my hips so tight I wouldn't be surprised if he leaves marks on me.

Slowly he starts to move my body against his, eliciting a groan from me as his cock slips from between my ass cheeks to the place I want it most. Fabric rubs across my sensitive bud, and I almost die from pleasure as sensation after sensation grips me.

"Too. Many. Clothes," he says through strangled breaths.

"Please, Finn. I need you."

Help me feel, I want to say. To erase the pain. The heartache of losing my father. The memory of losing you. I want to remember what it was like that night. Before everything went to shit.

"You have me," he states, ripping my pink lace thong from my body and thrusting into me to the hilt.

NINE

Willow

Waking up in Finn's arms is everything I imagined it would be and more. His warm body is wrapped around mine, his morning wood poking my lower back. My heart feels lighter. My thoughts dirtier. My cares about my heart breaking a distant memory as I lie awake and replay the events of last night.

The concern on his face when he first walked through my door. My hand throbbing in pain becoming minute compared to the ache in my core. The soar of my heart when we were texting while I waited for the doctor. Then the lust in his eyes as I undressed in front of him. The way his gaze heated my skin as he took in every inch of my skin.

But my favorite memory of last night ... the sweet words he whispered in my ear as he took me from behind. A contradiction to the pace he set which was urgent, needy. His goal clear as he worshiped my body with his hands while simultaneously punishing me with his cock. His words turned dirty the second round as I rode us through our second orgasms, slow and steady, both gasping for breath, sweat-slicked bodies sliding against one another until we jumped off the cliff together, flying high.

Best. Sex. Ever.

But I already knew that. I knew Finn was an amazing lover. A giver first, taking care of my needs before his own.

Nine months ago, I bit my lip so hard I drew blood trying to stay quiet. I was afraid my brother would hear us and burst through the door of Finn's bedroom. There was no doubt in my mind he would throttle him for touching me. Last night, neither of us held back.

Poor Kendall. I wouldn't be surprised if she heard every moan.

"Are you going to pretend to be asleep all day?" Finn asks, pulling my body closer to his, his large hand splayed across my stomach, drawing hearts on the exposed skin between my belly button and the valley of my breasts.

"Do we have to get up?"

I'm not ready to walk back into the real world. To face Kendall, or anyone else. I want to stay here with him, alone in my room, keep us in our little bubble just a little longer.

"We need to change your dressing."

Looking down at the white gauze the doctor wrapped around my finger as it rests against my pale-yellow sheet, I see there's a small, orangish discoloring where I know the gash is on my finger. I don't want to move, but he has a point. The sun is streaming through the blinds, telling me it's past time to get up, not that I have much on my plate today. I promised Evie I'd take her shopping for a prom dress, but otherwise my schedule is clear.

"I'm not ready," I whisper.

"It's day one of something great. We should get out of bed and enjoy it." Nuzzling his nose into my hair as he speaks, my heart warms. "And you stink."

"Way to kill the moment," I start, twisting in his arms to face him. I'm rewarded with a panty-melting smirk that sends jolts of electricity straight to where my panties would be if I were wearing any.

"Day one, LT."

I hear what he's saying but I hold back my smile. Riding his cock wasn't the only thing we did last night. We also talked. Which wasn't what I pictured us doing after having mind-blowing sex, but he insisted.

The short version of our conversation goes something like this …

No more dancing around each other. No more fighting what's between us. Because there is an *us*.

"Oh yeah? And what happens on day one?"

"Well, we've already taken care of the first thing on my list." Finn's smirk grows, his eyes darkening as he rolls on top of me, settling between my legs. "But I'd like to revisit that topic."

His touch is featherlight as his hands skate over my hips, down my thighs, and back up to where I want them the most. As soon as he brushes over my sensitive nub, I suck in a breath and hold it, waiting for more, but his hands still.

Just as I open my mouth to ask him why he stopped, he cuts me off. "And then, after I take care of you in every way possible, I'm going to have a talk with your brother."

My eyes widen in surprise, fear stabbing me in the heart. The deep V between Finn's eyebrows creases in concern.

"Maybe we should wait a little bit."

"You don't want to tell him?"

"I don't want him to kill you."

"He's not going to kill me, LT. I get that he's protective of you and Evie. You're his little sisters. No one will ever be good enough for you in his eyes. I agree with him, wholeheartedly. That's not going to stop me from trying to prove to him that I am. That I'll protect you, care for you, and love you. Every day."

Love me.

It's not the first time his choice of words has caused my heart to soar.

I've known Finn most of my life. He had one serious relationship, if you can call it that. He was a freshman in high school, and she was a senior. They lasted a little over six months. She took his virginity, and he took her to prom. He broke up with her that summer, shortly after summer break started. I haven't seen him date anyone since. Not seriously anyway. Though I doubt he's been celibate the whole time.

In fact, there's no way. Not with the skills he possesses.

"What if we wait a little while? Let him get used to me being around more."

"Like what? Hang out as *friends* when he's around?"

Letting out a sigh, I roll out from under him and throw back the covers. Curling my toes into the carpet as I stand, my nudity suddenly makes me self-conscious. I scan the floor for our discarded clothes. I can feel Finn's gaze on my backside, and as much as I like it, I know he'll distract me if I don't cover myself.

"I haven't been around much this year." After digging through my underwear drawer, I choose a sexy lace thong and slip it on quickly. "Maybe we should ease him into the idea." Silk shorts are next, followed quickly by a tank. When I'm fully dressed, I turn to face him. He's sitting up against my headboard, sheet pulled up around his waist, watching my every move. However, I can't read his eyes. His lips are firmly pressed together, the only indication he's not liking where this conversation is headed. "I'm not saying let's hide this from him forever, but it is still new for us. What if you change your mind next week?"

"I won't," he growls.

"You could possibly throw your friendship away for a quick fling."

"Not going to happen."

"Just think about it. There's no need to rush and tell everyone. Though, I'm sure Kendall is very aware of what we were doing last night." I feel the blush creep up in my cheeks, which brings a smile to his face.

"She better be, or I didn't do my job right."

Rolling my eyes, I take a seat on the edge of the bed next to him and cup his face with my good hand. "Look, I'm not going anywhere. I want this as much as you do.

It's all I've wanted for as long as I can remember. Why are you in such a rush to tell everyone?"

"Because you're mine, Willow. I want everyone to know that."

"I've been yours for years, Finn. Years. Let that sink in. That won't change. This ..." I say, motioning between us, the gauze streaking past his body catching my eye. The white a stark contrast to the color of his skin. "This is not about anyone else but us. Their opinion doesn't matter. But I'd hate for you to ruin your friendship with Max and we both know how his mind works. No matter when we decide to tell him, he's going to reject the idea. Why not let him see how much we care about each other? It might make it easier for him to accept this in the end."

Finn's only response is a growl before he captures my lips. His kiss is gentle but needy. I give him exactly what he needs, moving to straddle him, and he groans in appreciation when I grind against his growing erection.

"Keep doing that and I'm going to ruin your sheets," he warns, thrusting upward as he slows our kiss before pulling away. "You're afraid to tell him, aren't you?"

I nod as I attempt to get my breathing back under control.

"He's messed up right now, Finn. Losing my dad ..."

I don't have to finish the sentence. Finn's been by his side since Max got the call. He was there when he told me. Drove him home the next morning to be with my mother. Helped carry my father's casket.

Max and Finn have stood by each other's side since they were in diapers. The last thing I want is for this to ruin their friendship.

"No matter what he says, thinks, or does when we tell him, nothing will change the way I feel about you. If you want to wait a little while, I can do that, but I don't want to wait too long, LT. If he finds out from someone other than me or you, it'll make things harder. You do realize that, right?"

Again, I nod.

Because he's right. The longer we wait to tell him, the greater the chance people will figure out what's going on. The better the odds that he catches us. He needs to hear it from me. Or Finn, but preferably me. I want to tell Finn all of that, but I don't. Instead, I strip my clothes off and give him what he needs most.

Reassurance that I'm all in. That I feel the same way about him.

I give him my body, heart, and soul. Three things that have always been his.

After a shower, where round four consisted of me with my back pressed against the tiled walls, Finn and I finally dressed and left the safety of our little bubble. Thankfully, Kendall was nowhere to be found. A note on the counter in front of the coffee maker made it perfectly clear I wouldn't be able to escape her inquisition forever though.

LO,

Working until four, then I have an interview for the summer counselor gig. Meet me for dinner at The Bull at six. You have some explaining to do. No penis allowed.

XOXO - K

"I'm assuming that means I'm not invited," Finn jokes as he leans on the counter next to me.

"Considering you have a certain appendage, you would be correct. Lucky you. I can already hear the interrogation. I hope you're not shy because Kendall doesn't have a filter. She's going to ask questions that will make me blush."

Finn's burst of laughter sends shots of need to my core I try to ignore. The deep rumble of his voice, the way he throws his head back, his throat elongated, dampening my panties. He's so beautiful. But this morning it feels like I'm looking at him for the first time again. Noticing little details that I never have before.

Like how I fit perfectly against his body even though he's almost a foot taller than me. Or how when he smiles, the dimple in his chin is more prominent, even with his five o'clock shadow trying to hide it.

"Keep looking at me like that and we're never leaving this apartment again, LT. There are plenty of surfaces I haven't taken you on yet."

His damn dimple is smiling at me, and I can't help but press onto my tiptoes and kiss it.

"Sorry," I say, my voice lacking the apologetic tone it should hold. Because, let's be honest, if I could tie him up and keep him here, I would. In fact, tying him up sounds like a whole lot of fun.

"Coffee," he states, reading my mind. "You have to get on the road, and I need to make an appearance at my place. Max has already text me twice."

"What did you tell him?"

I swear my heart stops beating while I wait for him to answer.

"I told him I'd be there shortly. He's going to ask where I was, and I'm going to have to tell him something and I don't want to lie."

"Which means?"

"I won't lie to him. I'm going to tell him I was here. That Kendall called last night and needed me to take me you to the ER."

"Thirsty Thursday," I state.

"Huh?"

"He knows we have Thirsty Thursdays every week. He'll know we were drinking so Kendall couldn't drive me to the hospital. He also knows she'd never call him because she thinks he hates her."

"Is that why she texted me?" All I can do is nod because I honestly have no idea what K was thinking texting Finn last night. "If he's suspicious I'll show him the text."

"And if he asks where you slept or why you stayed?"

"I'm not going to lie to him, LT. I don't think he'll ask, but if he does, it was late, and I crashed in your bed. He's not going to ask if we had sex, I don't think he'll want to know the answer."

"Okay," I reply, the word coming out strangled as I attempt to control my breathing.

I can feel the beginning of a panic attack coming on at the thought of Max putting the pieces of the puzzle together before we have a chance to come clean with him. Black spots fill my vision the same way they did the night

Max told me about dad. I sway on my feet, gripping the counter with my good hand to steady myself.

When Finn wraps me in a warm embrace, my body immediately relaxes. The panic subsides faster than it ever has before.

TEN

Finn

Her hand was bandaged. The cut deeper than she thought. Stitches holding together her delicate skin. I wasn't about to leave her. I couldn't. My heart wouldn't let me. I had to see for myself that she had a fresh dressing in the morning, so it didn't get infected.

When I asked to stay the night, the last thing I thought would happen was a repeat of last summer. Not that I'm disappointed.

Hell, in my haste to be with Willow again, I fucking forgot a condom. I didn't even realize it at first, and once I did, I begged her not to make me stop. Thankfully, she didn't. Not my finest moment. But sinking into her sweet heat, it was like coming home again only better.

She was made just for me. Her body, her mind, her heart. They are mine. And I claimed her last night.

I wanted to go slow but there was no way I could, so instead I made sure she knew how I felt with my words as my body showed her. The second time was slower. The third, a welcome surprise after talking this morning. But my favorite moment from the last twenty-four hours was when I took her in the shower. When she begged for more. We talked more last night than we have in the last year. About how we feel. What we want. Not just from each other but in life. Today. Tomorrow. In the future. She wants to keep this from Max. I understand why, but at the same time I don't think she realizes how serious I am. I've said the words, showed her, but when she referred to herself as a fling, I wanted to punch the wall.

She could never be just a fling.

Still, when I get back to my loft, I avoid Max. I don't want to answer questions about where I was. If we don't talk about it, I don't have to lie to him. That doesn't stop him from seeking me out. Thankfully, it isn't to interrogate me, which makes me wonder if he even realizes I didn't stay here last night. I mean, he knew I wasn't home this morning.

"Party tomorrow night. Can you help me grab booze later?"

"Sure." You can hear the hesitation in my voice. Max isn't much of a partier. Yeah, we throw some kick ass get-togethers but we're both responsible. Neither of us drink more than we can handle, always maintaining a level of self-control.

"I need to let off some steam," he explains, reading my mind. "To focus on something else for a night. Just the guys. Nothing crazy. Julian said he'd bring over some food, which I was more than happy to pass off."

Max needs me to have his back right now and if getting drunk is what he wants to do, I'll let it slide … just this once. I'm going to keep my eye on him to make sure this doesn't turn into a habit. Alcohol is a nasty crutch to lean on. I don't want him to think he has nowhere else to turn, that he needs to drown his sorrow at the bottom of a bottle. It would be too easy for him to slide down that slippery slope.

———

Just the guys means all of our closest friends, including my brothers, and a few of the guys from the Kappa house, Max's fraternity. Don't get me wrong, those guys are okay. I have nothing against them, we just don't really click. Altogether, there are eight of us sitting around the poker table, drinking beer, and talking shit.

"Look at Finn's face," Declan says. "His hand is shit. I raise."

My hand is not shit, and him announcing that is his tell. A year younger than me, we used to play poker in our basement, and I always crushed him. Micah, on the other hand, is cool as a cucumber as he stares at me, attempting to read my blank face. Of the three of us, he may be the youngest, but he has the best poker face.

"I'm out," everyone but Declan and Julian announce.

Oh yeah, Julian has a stick up his ass tonight. He hasn't won a single hand yet. We're only playing with quarters but they're adding up. We each started with a roll, ten dollars of silver, and he's down to his last three. He just doesn't know when to fold.

The three of us show our hands, and Declan's smile deflates. My four of a kind trumps his straight and Julian's full house. They groan in unison as Max pushes away from the table, stumbling a little. Everyone's eyes fall to him while he staggers down the hall toward his room. Looking around, I see the uncertainty in everyone's eyes. No one knows what to do or how to react right now. They've never seen Max like this before. Hell, I've only seen him drunk a handful of times and it was when we were younger, before we realized the buzz was more fun than the hangover.

He needs a reminder of that right now.

"I've got him," Dec and I say at the same time.

The rest of our friends follow at a safe distance as we make our way into Max's room, rounding his bed, and heading into his adjoining bath. I don't think anyone is prepared for what we find.

Max with a bottle of whiskey. Sitting on the floor next to the toilet, leaning back against the bathtub. His eyes are closed but tears are streaming down his face as he silently cries into the bottle as he takes another gulp.

After sharing a look with Dec, he corrals our friends back into the living room. Taking a seat next to my best friend, I lean back against the tub, stretching out my legs. Neither of us say anything, knowing words won't take away the pain. They won't change his situation. When he passes me the whiskey, I take a sip, the warm amber liquid burning its way down my throat, before setting it aside.

"I was drinking that," Max states, his words slurred.

"The buzz is better than the hangover."

"The buzz doesn't ease the pain," he retorts, opening his eyes and glaring at me.

"Nothing will." Staring into the depths of Max's blue eyes, the same blue eyes his sisters have, an ache settles in my chest. He's broken and no amount of alcohol will ease the pain.

Closing his eyes again, Max slumps against my shoulder. His tears soak the sleeve of my shirt as we sit there in silence until I hear the soft sounds of Max snoring. Reaching into my pocket, I pull out my phone and text Declan for help. Together, we lift Max off the floor and into his bed.

"I love you, Dad," he mumbles softly as I pull the sheets over him.

My heart breaks all over again for my best friend as I stare down at him. My mouth opens to answer him, wanting him to know his father loves him as well, when Declan's hand lands on my damp shoulder.

"Don't, man. He won't even remember in the morning."

If only he could forget the last week as easily as he'll forget the last hour.

ELEVEN

Willow

"I'm so jealous," Kendall swoons. "Why can't I find a guy like Finn? Romantic. Sweet. Hot as fuck. Makes you scream him name—"

"Stop," I beg when her voice starts to rise.

We're sitting at a table in the middle of our favorite dive bar, The Bull, around the corner from our apartment, sharing a plate of greasy cheese fries while we wait for our salads to arrive. This is Kendall's version of a balanced meal.

Artery clogging food, a healthy—dressing on the side —plate of greens, washed down with water or diet soda.

Piper's tried to explain how unhealthy K's diet is on multiple occasion. She's studying nutrition and works at the health and wellness center on campus, hoping to one day counsel young minds. After struggling with bulimia when she was in high school because she was bullied for being overweight, she's going to make a great role model for those struggling with the same issues.

K's not bulimic by any means. Or overweight. She rocks her curves, proud of her body. She eats whatever she wants but puts in the work so she can indulge. We both do.

"Look, all I'm saying is that you two are cute. You deserve to be treated like a damn princess, and that's exactly what he's doing. And rocking your world on top of it. I don't understand why you want to keep this a secret."

She knows why.

We spent the better part of twenty minutes discussing it while we waited for the fries to arrive.

"Max is going to freak out. I just know it, and the last thing I want is for there to be tension between him and Finn, or worse, to ruin their friendship. He won't be able to handle it right now. He wants people to think he's handling Dad's death fine, but I know my brother. He's masking his feelings and putting up a good front."

"If your brother really loves you, he'll get over it. He might be a hard-headed asshole most of the time, but he wants you to be happy."

The waitress arrives with our salads, cutting off my hesitant reply. Is that all Max wants? For me to be happy? If that's the case, he'll have to accept my relationship with Finn because I'm happier than I've ever been.

While I was shopping with Evie this afternoon, I made some startling realizations about life.

1. It's too short to not be happy.
2. If I were to write a dictionary, under the word perfect would be a picture of Finn.
3. I'm still grieving the loss of my father, but he wouldn't want me to stop living just because he's no longer here.

I'm fairly certain that was the most encompassing thought of my afternoon. Because my father lived to make his children smile. To brighten our day. To bask in the joy we brought him.

Watching Evie as she went through the motions of trying on dress after dress only drove my realization deeper. After she finally picked out a way-too-revealing-for-my-liking black dress, one that is guaranteed to make Max lose his shit if he sees her in it, I took her out for ice cream. Her grief was written all over her face while I was internalizing mine.

There's only two years between us but she's one of my closest friends. Yes, she's my sister, she's still young and figuring out who she is, but I've always treated her as my equal. In a little less than a month she'll graduate from high school, and this fall she'll be joining me and Max at Lake State as a freshman. These should be some of the happiest days of her life but they're not.

"You know," I started as she poked at her waffle bowl of Superman ice cream, her favorite, "Dad wouldn't want you to be sad."

"Yeah, well, he's not here so he doesn't have a say." Her words are filled with venom, anger.

"You're right, he's not. He would be if he could. You and I both know that. There was nothing he wouldn't do for us, to make us happy." She doesn't reply or look up from her ice cream, but I know she heard me. I can see the tears in her eyes she's trying to contain. "Do you remember your fifth birthday?"

She shakes her head, wiping away a stray tear.

"You wanted a My Little Pony Party. Everything was

pink. I thought it was the coolest because that was my favorite color. Max was teasing you because he said you were copying me. Do you know what Dad did, so you'd stop crying?" I pause, giving her a chance to picture the party in her mind. She may not remember it now but it's a day I'll never forget. It was the day I realized my little sister looked up to me. I was only seven, but I felt like the coolest person in the universe. "He raided the closets for anything pink that would fit Max and made him wear the outfit all day. He didn't care that it would embarrass him. Or that my shorts were really tight on him. Or that it was the middle of winter and Max looked like he was going to the beach. All he wanted to do was make you smile because it was your special day."

"I don't remember any of that," she says, finally looking up.

"Mom has pictures somewhere unless Max found them and burned them."

"I'll kill him," she mumbles around a huge bite of her pink, yellow, and blue ice cream.

"You should have seen your smile, Evie. It was so bright. Dad loved it when you smiled. He lived for it. All he wanted was for us to be happy. To not have to worry about things like money. To enjoy our childhood, experience life, and have the freedom to figure out who we are. He may not be here physically, but he'll always be *here*," I state, placing my hand over my heart, "and he still wants all those things for us. He wants us to smile, even though we hurt. To live, even though it feels like we can't go on. To do what makes us happy."

Fresh tears form in the corners of her eyes, and this

time, she doesn't shy away when they spill over. Reaching across the table, I pull her hand in mine and gave it a tiny squeeze.

"I'm here for you whenever you need me. A phone call away."

I felt her anger and grief lighten, even if only a little, after that. Baby steps. There is no timeline on grieving. We all work through it differently. How I feel today may take Evie weeks or even years. I'll be there with her every step of the way though. As long as she knows that she's going to be okay. We both are.

"You okay?" Kendall asks, visions of Evie's grief-stricken face fading away. "You're crying, Lo. Want to talk about it?"

Wiping away the tears I didn't realize had fallen, I take a deep breath and let it out slowly.

"Evie and I went dress shopping today."

"How's she doing?"

"Not great, but I think maybe a little better than she was yesterday. We had a nice long talk and it helped, at least a little."

"And what about you? How are you doing?"

It feels like everyone keeps asking me and I still don't have an answer for them. If I say I'm *fine*, I get a look of disbelief. If I say I'm *good*, I feel like I'm lying. I want to joke and say I'm still alive, but I have a feeling that won't go over well. Not in my circle. Especially not with people like Kendall and Finn.

"I'm okay. I have my moments, that's for sure, but our talk helped me, too. Being back home was the hardest part. I couldn't even bring myself to go in the house when I dropped her off."

"You didn't see your mom?" The look of shock on Kendall's face makes me roll my eyes. She knows how close I am with my mom. As close if not closer than I was with my dad.

"She was out front planting flowers."

"How'd she look?"

"About the same. You could tell she'd been crying, but she's doing everything she can to stay busy, going through the motions, trying to get back to her normal routine a little more each day. I'm glad Evie's there but I'm worried about when Evie leaves this fall. She'll be all alone in that house, surrounded by memories. At Christmas they were talking about taking a trip, a second honeymoon, once they were empty nesters. I can't imagine it's going to be easy on her."

I'd been helping my dad plan the perfect getaway for them. A redo of their original honeymoon, where Max was conceived. The entire trip was a shit show, from a hurricane causing them to shelter in place for two days, to missing luggage, my mother losing her purse, and the toilet in their room breaking. They claimed it was one of the most adventurous trips they'd ever been on and said if they could survive that, they could survive anything.

I have no doubt they would have. This August would have been their twenty-third anniversary.

"We can all takes turns visiting her," I continue. "Evie's going to park her car here since she can't have it on campus. One of us will go back every weekend, maybe a night in the middle of the week if our schedules allow.

I'll talk to her friends, too. She has book club and stuff to keep her busy, but it'll be the first time in a long time where she doesn't have someone to take care of, ya know?"

My mother lives for her family the same way my dad did. She gave up her career to take care of us. To raise her children. To make sure dinner was on the table when dad got home from work and that our homework was done every night. I'm worried she'll feel like her purpose is gone when we need her more than anything now.

"Have you told her about Finn?"

"No. You're the only one who knows, and you can't tell anyone." Pointing at K with my fork, my voice is stern. She holds back a laugh. I know she won't tell anyone, not even Piper or Alexis, but I'm freaking out at the thought anyway. "I almost told Evie today, but I changed my mind. I don't want to put her in the awkward position of keeping it from Max."

"You should just tell Max. Rip off the band-aid. Let him freak out. He'll get over it eventually."

"Not exactly how his mind works," I mutter, shoving a crouton in my mouth.

"Well, if you're not going to tell him you need to be careful. He's not blind, Lo, and you suck at lying. Anyone with a brain can see the attraction between you and Finn. It's been obvious for years. Now that you've both pulled your heads out of your asses, it's going to be even harder to deny when you're in the same room."

Shit!

She's right. Max is going to see right through us. My eyes have always been drawn to Finn anytime he's in the same room as me. I feel his presence before I see him. I'm pulled into his orbit, always moving closer until I can smell the fresh mint from his gum or the hint of sandalwood from his bodywash.

"I'm so screwed," I state, dropping my fork onto the plate with a clatter.

"No, last night you were screwed," she says with a laugh. "Look, it's going to be fine. And even if he is pissed, he can either get over himself or ..." Her voice drifts off as she looks over my shoulder.

"Or what?" I ask when she doesn't continue.

"What?" she echoes.

"You said he could get over himself or ..."

"Oh," she starts, shaking her head as if to clear her mind. "Yeah, I don't know."

Glancing behind me, I look around the crowded entrance to the restaurant to see if I can spot anyone I know. Whoever caught Kendall's eye. When I turn back to face her, she's blushing, her head down as she quickly demolishes the last of her salad.

I've obviously missed something.

"Anything you want to share with the rest of the table?" I ask as I hear her phone chime.

"What do you mean?"

She's a worse liar than I am. Her voice is laced with guilt and panic.

"Who is he, K? I saw the expression on your face."

"No one," she denies, her phone chiming again.

"Why don't you answer your phone then?"

"We're eating dinner. I can check it later."

"What if it's important?"

"It's probably not." Tossing her napkin on her empty plate, Kendall stands, rubbing her tattoo. "I'm going to use the bathroom. Will you order me a cheesecake?"

She's walking away before I can agree. I don't think she realizes she gives away as much as she does with her body language. Normally her head is held high, shoulders back, each step taken with purpose. She's fearless in everything she does. However, as I watch her walk toward the hall leading to the restrooms, I notice the slight slump of her shoulders and the fever in her steps.

Yeah, there's a guy. She might not be ready to tell me about him yet, but he exists. I'm certain of it.

TWELVE

Willow

It's been two days since I've seen Finn. Not that I haven't had the chance. If I'm being honest with myself, I've been avoiding him. I don't even know why.

I want to be with him. There's no doubt in my mind.

Still, me being elusive doesn't stop him from texting me every day.

I'm shoving a Twix bar in mouth, fighting the urge to ask him to come over, when my phone chimes. My heart skips a beat imagining that it's Finn. Did he know I was thinking about him?

MAX: Hey, haven't talked to you in a few days. Wanted to check in. You doing okay?
ME: Yeah, fine. How are you?
MAX: Okay. Got a little drunk last night with the guys, might have broken down in the bathroom, but I'll deny it if you say anything. Otherwise, I'm okay.
ME: You know, I'm always here if you wanna talk. Dad would want us to keep moving forward. In fact, I think he'd be pissed if we wallowed anymore.

I give Max a shortened version of what I said to Evie. She's younger, more emotional. Max doesn't need me to tiptoe around his feelings.

MAX: Are you listening to your own advice?
ME: Trying. I know it's not easy, but I'm taking it one day at a time. It's all we can do.

God, why do I sound so insightful. He's normally the one giving me advice. Pushing me through the darkness. Now, here I am, in the midst of the hardest situation we've had to deal with, standing strong. And I feel strong.

Death is hard. You always wish you had said *I love you* one more time. Spent more time together. Given them a longer hug or made more of an effort to call even if you were busy.

I'm lucky because those are not things I'm worried about. My relationship with my dad was amazing. Our bond was strong. I know he loved me. He didn't have to call me every day just to reinforce that. We spent as much time together as our crazy lives allowed.

Am I devastated he's not here anymore to talk to? To ask advice. To wrap me in a hug when I'm on the verge of a breakdown or panic attack?

Of course.

But if I allow myself to dwell on it instead of rise above the pain, he would be pissed at me.

I know this because my father was not only Max's hero but also mine, and I was his mini-me. Yes, Max looked more like him, their voice has the same timbre, and their look of disapproval is scarily similar, but I was the one who grew up wanting to be just like my dad. Family man—or in my case, woman—and successful lawyer.

After I turned sixteen, he let me work in his law office a few days a week that summer, filing paperwork, answering phones. He allowed me to help him research from time to time, teaching me how to use the thick law books he kept on the bookshelves in his office. And when he was preparing for court, I was his jury. He practiced his opening remarks and asked me to give him a verdict based on how he presented the case.

One day, I'd love nothing more than to have the same kind of relationship with a child of my own. That summer brought us closer together. The hours were long, the tedious work I was allowed to do boring, but we ate lunch together every day I was there. It's time I'll always cherish. Something that was just between us.

MAX: Want to come over for dinner tonight? Finn says he's making a huge spread and that we need to invite people. Brady and Julian will be here, I think.

He is, is he? How convenient.

ME: Can I bring Kendall?
MAX: Do you have to?
ME: I don't get why you don't like her. She's always been nice to you. Hell, she tiptoes around you because even she can tell you don't like her.
MAX: I don't dislike her she's just loud. And when she

drinks, which she normally does when she's here, she's even louder.

ME: Please.

MAX: Bring whoever you want. I know you normally study with your friends on Sundays, but I wasn't sure what you had planned since you're not taking summer classes.

Well, I was until I decided to drop them at the last minute. The last thing I wanted to worry about were my grades right now. I wasn't sure how much my grief would consume me, and with summer classes being intense, I quickly withdrew.

ME: No plans tonight. What time?

MAX: Come on over whenever you want. Finn's in the shower, and then I think he's going to start cooking. If you're here maybe you can help him, so I don't have to.

Vivid images of Finn with water glistening off his bare chest, damn hair, and wearing only an apron cloud my vision. It's a sight I can't unsee. Hell yes, I'll help him in the kitchen!

ME: Doesn't Julian want to be a chef? Can't you rope him into helping?

There, I don't sound so eager to help.

MAX: Julian has something going on with baseball.

Won't be here until later. Why do you think we're letting Finn cook instead of him?
ME: Fine. I'll help cook, but that means you have to entertain everyone else. Including Kendall. And you have to be nice to her.
MAX: Deal. See you soon.

Kendall walks in the living room just as I set my phone aside. Looking from me to the open bag of fun-sized candy bars, she lifts her eyebrow in question.

"I only ate a few," I say defensively as I start to clean up the wrappers that are scattered all over the coffee table.

"Sure. Is that why the bag is almost empty?"

My addiction to all things chocolate, but mostly Twix bars, is not a secret. Once I open the bag, I lose all self-control.

"Max invited us over for dinner," I state, avoiding her rhetorical question.

"Max invited *us* over. Are you sure?"

"Yes." Avoiding her curious gaze, I head into my room, stopping to drop my wrappers in the garbage on the way. Kendall's on my heels the entire time.

"That doesn't sound like your brother at all. Inviting me anywhere."

"Technically he invited me and said I could bring whoever I wanted with me. I choose you, bestie. Now, put on something nice and let's get out of here."

"Why do I have to wear something nice? Is this not good enough for dinner with your family?" she asks, gesturing to her black yoga pants and holey, oversized T-shirt.

"It's a dinner party."

"Ooh," she says dramatically before rolling her eyes. "Okay. Are we talking black tie, or can I just slip on some jeans?"

"Jeans and a clean shirt will be fine."

With a nod, she spins and leaves me to get changed. Jeans, check. Fresh makeup, check. Body spray I know Finn likes, double check. Searching my closet for a cute top to wear, that I'm not afraid to get dirty while cooking, I feel my phone vibrate in my back pocket.

FINN: I hear you're helping me cook tonight.
ME: Max chose me as the sacrifice, so he doesn't have to help.
FINN: Remind me to thank him later.
ME: Ha ha. We'll be there in twenty minutes tops. Need us to pick up anything?
FINN: Condoms?

Yeah, those are probably a good idea considering we have a hard time keeping our hands off each other. Then again, if we don't have them, maybe we'll behave better in front of Max.

Who am I kidding? The first time we had sex the other night he didn't use one. Thankfully I've been on the pill for years and never forget to take it. Not having protection didn't stop us then, and available or not, if given the opportunity, Finn and I will still go at it.

ME: I can grab some if you're serious, but you have to keep your hands, and your cock, to yourself tonight.

> I'm still not ready to tell Max. He's not ready to hear it.
>
> FINN: I know. He's been walking around like a zombie most of the day, hence the dinner party.
>
> ME: Are you sure he wasn't just hungover?

He said he was fine. That he got drunk last night. If he's not coping well, I want to be there for him. Why would he lie to me?

> FINN: He was but that wasn't his hungover face I was seeing. Why?
>
> ME: Tell you later. See you in a few.

Stubborn. Hard-headed. Stupid fucking Max.

He's trying to be so strong for the rest of us that he's not taking care of himself. And that's going to stop today. Because Dad would be irate if he knew Max was walking around like a zombie. He'd give him one hell of a lecture and kick his ass into gear.

Which means that's up to me if it's as bad as Finn has me thinking it might be.

Thirty minutes later, with a bottle of wine in each had, Kendall and I arrive at Max and Finn's loft. Brady's already here, judging by the choice in music. Hard rock blares through the surround sound speakers at an almost deafening level. When he appears in the hall, a look of irritation on his face, still in his black leather jacket, I'm not surprised.

Stomping over to the entertainment system, he lowers the volume before shrugging out of his jacket and tossing it on the couch. Kendall and I both watch in awe of his graceful moves.

Brady's a hottie for sure. Six-foot tall, beautiful gray eyes, clean cut but with a bad boy vibe. Tattoo's cover both of his arms. His right is a full sleeve, and his left will be when it's finished. Right now, the ink stops just above his elbow. And the best part ... he drives a Harley. Not that I'm allowed to ride on it with him. Max shut that down years ago. My dad backed him up on it.

I've known Brady since he moved to our sleepy little town in high school. He hit it off with Finn quick, helping Finn rebuild his car. Max and him seem to have a love hate relationship sometimes. They get along great but like to fight each other. Mostly with snarky comments, calling each other names, but fists have flown a few times.

"Lo!" Brady exclaims when he finally catches sight of us, rushing over and pulling me into his arms. "Your brother's being a little bitch tonight."

"Isn't he always?" Kendall whispers as he pulls her in for a hug.

I tried fixing them up at the beginning of last summer. They mix about as well as oil and water. Kendall's too high maintenance for him. Brady's too laid back, go with the flow for her. So instead of dating, they became great friends.

"Don't I know it," he says as he takes a bottle of wine from each of us. "Do you really think we needed four bottles?"

"Well, from what I was told, there's going to be at least six of us at some point. Piper and Alexis might come but they didn't want to commit to anything. Both of them are taking summer classes that start tomorrow and you know how they are. Probably studying already."

Brady's hella smart, too. Not many people know it, because he doesn't flaunt it, but he was the valedictorian of his graduating class. He could have gone to school anywhere but had moved so much growing up, he was sick of starting over so he came here with Finn and Max. I'm sure the scholarship he was offered didn't hurt either.

One day I might be calling him Doctor Coleman. He's studying pre-med but not sure what he really wants to do with it.

"Too bad. Those girls are fun to talk to. What about your sister, K? Why isn't she here?"

A giggle bubbles in my throat and I swallow it, covering my mouth just in case.

If there's one person Max detests more than Kendall, it's her twin sister, Kora. They can't even be in the same room as each other without getting into a verbal altercation. Which makes life interesting when Kora hangs out with us.

"She's working as a flight attendant this summer. She wanted to travel the world before she graduated college, and so she's doing it and getting paid. My mom did the same thing when she was our age."

"That's dope as fuck. Where is she right now?"

Kendall and Brady migrate toward the kitchen, deep in conversation. I follow, wondering where Max and Finn are hiding. As soon as I step around the corner, I have my answer.

"Thank God," Max exclaims, immediately tugging the strings on the black apron he's wearing, whipping the fabric over his head, and tossing it at me in one swift motion.

"Hello to you, too, big brother." He pulls me in for a hug, kisses my cheek, and then disappears into the living room without another word.

"Hey," Finn says, his eyes traveling the length of my body, leaving a prickle of heat in their path, as he takes in my outfit.

I kept it simple with dark, skinny jeans and a low-cut white blouse with bright yellow daisies on it. I figured the jeans would hide the stains, and I could bleach the shirt if I spilled anything on it. Or toss it. I'm not that attached to it.

When his eyes flick back to mine, the corner of his mouth lifts in a dangerous smile.

Checking behind me to make sure Max isn't around, I notice we're completely alone. Kendall and Brady slipped out at some point. Reaching into my back pocket, I pull out the one condom I had in my nightstand and toss it to him. He catches it with ease and lifts his eyebrow at me.

"Just in case," I state, setting my purse on the island before sliding the apron over my head. "What's on the menu tonight?"

"You."

THIRTEEN

Willow

Cooking with Finn is the most fun I've had in a long time. We move like a perfectly choreographed dance as we work. I tackle the appetizers and salad while Finn sets up the steaks to marinate and begins working on side dishes.

Fresh bruschetta on toasted French baguette to start. Twice baked potatoes, green beans, and a garden salad with my favorite crunchy sunflower seed topping as the sides.

"Potatoes have another ten minutes and then I'll start the steaks," Finn says as I begin pulling down plates.

"It smells amazing in here."

When he doesn't reply, I look over my shoulder to see his eyes smoldering in my direction. "Yes, it does."

Max rounds the corner before I can reply. Finn immediately turns to face the stove again, but I don't miss the way he slightly adjusts himself as he does.

"How much longer are you two planning on torturing me?" he asks, twisting the cork in a fresh bottle of wine.

What?

Did he see the look Finn gave me? Does he know what's going on? Did Finn talk to him without telling me? He wouldn't do that, would he? We agreed to wait. I want to be the one to tell Max. When the time's right. After things calm down. When I know he can handle it.

"What's wrong with you?" Max quirks his eyebrow at me when I don't answer. He holds my stare for a few beats before Finn butts in, drawing his attention away from me.

"Thirty minutes, man. Tops. I'm about to start the steaks."

"Cool. My stomach's been making some interesting noises for almost an hour."

Without so much as a backwards glance, Max heads back to the living room. Julian showed up a few minutes ago, popping in the kitchen to say hello and offering help which Finn quickly dismissed. Julian's studying to go to culinary school. His love for cooking trumps everything except baseball. He's been the starting pitcher for LSU since his freshman year.

Finn and I work in silence as we finish dinner. He excuses himself to his room as all of our friends gather around the island, filling their plates. When he doesn't return after ten minutes, I head in search of him, claiming I need to use the restroom.

His bedroom door is wide open, and Finn is seated at the edge of his bed, head in his hands.

"Whatcha doing?" I ask as I casually lean against the doorjamb.

"Freaking out a little," he states as he lifts his head, his eyes searching mine for answers I don't have.

"Aren't you supposed to be the overly confident one between the two of us?" I joke, moving into the room and sitting next to him.

"I just don't want to screw this up."

"You're not going to. We have a solid plan. All we have to do is stick to it."

And by solid plan I mean we decided to wait until the time was right to tell Max about us. To act casual and avoid staring at each other.

"My dick was pressed against the stove the entire time we were cooking, and I didn't even touch you, LT. Your scent alone was enough to make me hard. And then when he came for more wine, I thought we were busted. My cock was so hard by that point I was worried about popping the button off my jeans."

I can't help the giggle that escapes. I'm picturing buttons flying across the kitchen, coming from his crotch. His jeans falling to his ankles as his cock stands at attention, pointing at me.

"Not as funny as you think," he snorts. It's the cutest thing. He's trying really hard not to laugh at the image I'm sure is in his head as well. Finally, he glances at me, and I can see the smile he's unable to contain. "You think they'd notice if we didn't eat dinner?"

"Sadly, yes," I state.

Groaning, Finn stands, extending his hand to me. When I place my palm in his, he tugs me close to his body, wrapping his arms around me. "Thank you for helping me cook tonight. I really appreciate it."

"It was fun."

"Just think, someday that will be what we do every

night. Only, if I have my way, you won't be wearing any clothes under your apron."

"A shiver runs up my spine as his words sink in, a reflection of the images I conjured of him earlier.

"You guys coming?" Brady hollers down the hall. "Food's getting cold."

"Be right there," I shout, stepping out of Finn's warm embrace. "We better get back out there before people start to talk."

"They've been talking about us for years, LT."

"No, they haven't," I say, nudging his shoulder as we walk down the hall.

"Yes, they have. It's not a secret how I feel about you because I never wanted it to be." Pulling me to a stop just before we get to the end of the hall and in view of all our friends, Finn whispers in my ear, "And you, gorgeous, have a hard time keeping your eyes off of me."

Screw food. All I want right now is Finn, naked. His hand on me, his mouth covering mine, thrusting into me so deep I can't catch my breath.

"Finally," Max states, irritation clear as he stares at us, his eyes dropping to our hands. That's when I realize our fingers are still laced together.

Pulling away will make us look guilty. Continuing to hold his hand would give Max a reason to ask questions.

Finn makes the decision for us, casually releasing my hand and slinging his arm over my shoulder.

"So? How'd we do? Positive feedback welcome. Negative feedback means you're not invited next time."

Nice change of direction, Finn. He's acting casual, as if nothing is wrong. However, I can feel the tension in his body as he speaks. He's strung as tight as I am right now. He didn't miss the way Max was looking at us. The accusation in his eyes.

Kendall giggles, holding up her finger as she chews. "Everything is great."

Brady and Julian chime in with compliments of their own. All eyes fall to Max when he remains silent, still staring in our direction.

"Well?" I ask him. "What do you think? I even put the crunchy stuff on the salad we both love."

"It's good. What took you so long?" he finally asks.

"We were giving you guys some time to dig in," Finn says. "*Someone* was worried you guys wouldn't like the food even though she rocked as my co-chef."

"It's called a sous chef," Julian chimes in, his voice strained.

Dropping his arm from around my shoulder, Finn turns to fully face Julian, crossing his arms over his chest. "Fine, she was a terrific sous chef."

"If you want to pretend to know what you're doing at least know the lingo. Have you ever even worked in a restaurant?"

Oh, shit. Here we go.

"Don't need to. My mama taught me how to cook and she's the real deal."

"I didn't realize your mom was a chef. I thought that was my mom. Oh, wait. My mom *is* a chef."

Stepping between them, I hold out my hands and shake my head. "Unnecessary. Everyone shut up and eat."

The only noise for the next thirty minutes is the scrape of forks across plates followed by the clatter of dishes as they're loaded into the dishwasher. After the kitchen is cleaned up and all four bottles of wine are polished off, Kendall and I say our good-byes.

Finn's hug is brief while Max seems to hold onto me longer than usual.

"Call me later," he whispers in my ear. "I want to talk to you about something."

I'm sure he does. More than likely the fact I was holding hands with his best friend.

All I do is nod against his shoulder and step back, avoiding eye contact. It makes me look guilty, but I don't stop myself. I am guilty. I feel guilty. I don't like lying to my brother and I'm terrible at it. One look at me and he'll know everything I'm thinking.

"Well, that was interesting," Kendall says as she slips into the passenger seat of my car.

"Big or small, any gathering at Max's tends to be interesting."

"Not what I meant," she says after I pull away from the curb, heading toward our apartment. I can tell she's had a few too many glasses of wine, which means her lips are looser than normal. I prefer to be right there with her when she's like this, but I barely finished one glass.

"Okay, I'll bite. What did you mean?"

"Do you really think Julian is that stuck up? That he wasn't poking at Finn to distract Max?"

The thought crossed my mind, but I brushed it off. Those two argue over food more than any two people I've ever met. Yes, Julian's mother is a professional chef, and he certainly has her talent, but Finn is no slouch in the kitchen. He can hold his own. I always preferred family dinners at his house over ours when we'd get together. Mary, Finn's mom, is a wonderful cook, and I loved watching her teach Finn.

"Do you think Max is on to us already?"

"I think Max has been on to you guys for years but now that you're actually a thing, it's hard not to see the subtle changes in your relationship. To feel the shift. You guys need to tell him sooner rather than later. The longer you wait the harder it's going to be and the angrier he's going to get when he finds out you've been keeping it a secret from him."

Fuck!

We need a better plan.

As soon as we're home, I shoot Finn a text to let him know.

FINN: Thanks again for cooking with me tonight.
ME: Anytime.

How do I start this conversation with him without freaking him out? I don't think there is a way. It's not like I want to break up with him, if that's even something I could do at this point. It's not like we put a title on what's going on between us though the things he says to me make me wonder if we need one.

I'm his. Nothing else matters.

And for all intents and purposes, he's mine. Or at least I want him to be.

ME: We need to talk. (yes, I know how that sounds but I couldn't figure out how else to say it)

FINN: Do you want me to come over for this?
ME: I'd rather not do it over text.
FINN: Give me an hour. I don't want to leave yet. Max is watching me like a hawk. I've been showing him stupid cat memes so he didn't get suspicious why I was on my phone.
ME: That's exactly what we need to talk about. We're busted.
FINN: Thirty minutes. He's headed to bed. I want to be alone with you anyway.
ME: Just don't make it obvious.
FINN: I'm staying the night.
ME: That would make it obvious.
FINN: Still staying. See you in a bit, love.

Damn him. He's going to get caught and then what?

Oh, by the way, Max, we've been humping like bunnies for a while now. Thought you should know.

Max is going to kill him.

Punctual as always, thirty minutes later I hear the rumble of Sasha's engine outside. Opening the front door, I watch as he climbs the stairs, taking them two at a time. When he sees me standing in the doorway, his grin grows.

"Well, hello, beautiful. Are you waiting for me?"

"Are you the stripper I ordered? You look nothing like your picture," I joke.

Finn growls, lifting me and throwing me over his shoulder when he reaches me, causing me to let out a little yelp. Kicking the door shut as I beat against his back, I'm careful not to use too much force so I don't bust a stitch.

"Put me down," I beg, but he doesn't stop until he's in my room, the door slamming closed behind him.

Slowly, he lowers me to the ground, my body sliding against his.

"You want to talk?" he asks.

His brown eyes are almost black, swirling with emotions as he stares down at me. Lust. Need. Longing. The same feelings that are consuming me right now. Causing my heart to beat a thunderous rhythm against my ribcage.

I can't think of a single question I want to ask him right now.

"Nope," I finally say, popping the *P* for emphasis.

"Good." Reaching to the nape of his neck, Finn pulls his T-shirt over his head, tossing it aside. "There's something else I'd rather do right now anyway."

"Oh, yeah?" I challenge, taking a step back only for him to match me.

"Yeah. You."

His lips land on mine, and all thoughts of Max and being caught are a distant memory. Nothing matters when I'm in his arms. When his lips are one mine. When my heart beats in sync with his, the way it's doing right now.

FOURTEEN

Finn

Sneaking over to LT's place was easier than I thought it would be. Max was already in his room, more than likely asleep. He woke up with a hangover but even after that seemed to fade, he was still walking around in a daze. Having people over for dinner helped brighten his mood slightly. Until Willow and I spent a little too much time away from the rest of our group.

Oops.

I didn't mean for her to follow me. I just needed a minute to compose myself. I'd had a raging hard-on since she walked in the door. I missed seeing her the past few days, and her scent alone was enough to bring back fond memories of what we did that night. Multiple times. With her screaming my name.

Hence the boner I was sporting.

Her tossing me a condom was meant to be playful but only compounded my issue. I wanted nothing more than to sheath myself and bend her over the kitchen island. I didn't give a shit who walked in on us. Or that her brother was in the next room.

Being around her and not being able to touch her was pure torture, so as soon as the food was finished, I went to my room so I could have a second to breathe. To calm myself down. To adjust the bulge in my pants. I should have locked myself in the bathroom and taken care of matters. It would have been quick, too. Three pumps, maybe four. Like when I was teenager and learned how amazing masturbation was.

Now, she wants to talk.

Am I scared? Not really.

We're on the same page. I know how she feels about me, or at least I have an idea. This isn't one of those we-need-to-talk conversations that generally signifies the death of a relationship. No, I'm fairly sure she wants to talk about Max and that's fine. I have a few concerns of my own about her brother, mainly the fact he's headed down a dark path that I want nothing more than to save him from.

However, as soon as I walk through the door, my little tree gets sassy with me, my blood heats in my veins, and the last thing I want to do is talk about her brother or our relationship. It's a damn good thing my girl and I are on the same page. We don't need words to communicate how we feel.

Every night I wait for Max to close himself in his room before I sneak out. I've started wearing running clothes so at least it looks like I have a reason to be up when I return the next morning as the sun's starting to rise, sweat covering my body. Sometimes he's awake, sometimes he doesn't pull himself out of bed until after I've showered.

Max has been quiet, more so than normal. Inside of his own head. I know he's trying to figure shit out but I'm starting to get worried. I think it's more than just his dad's death that's weighing on him. More than losing him. He won't talk about it. I've tried, but he changes the topic of conversation.

He finds a way to avoid talking about it with me by inviting the guys over for poker or Willow and Kendall over for dinner. He'll put on a good show, act like he's back to normal, but then when it's just the two of us again, he closes himself in his room. I've been checking his room for hidden liquor bottles when he's out to make sure he isn't hiding more than just his feelings.

I'm afraid to tell Willow how bad he's gotten. How far he's fallen. Max is the epitome of strength. He's the protector. A leader. The person walking around our loft the last week is not my best friend.

All my research says to just be available. That everyone grieves differently. If he turns to drugs or alcohol to cope, I'll step in. Until then, I've been casually making my presence known. Engaging him in meaningless conversation.

I'm starting to wonder if blurting out that I'm screwing his sister is the only thing that will shake him out of his haze. I know it would do the trick, but that's not really the way I want to tell him, and even though I've spent every night with Willow, held her in my arms, woken her up with my lips against her neck, we still haven't decided when or how to tell Max about us.

Because there is an us. There is no denying that.

And now, adding to his stress level, is Evie's prom

date. Joe's a good kid. He grew up down the street, has always treated Evie with respect, but that doesn't mean Max is going to let him take her out without giving her *the speech* the way James would have if he were still here. Nope, Max is taking on that responsibility.

I remember when James gave both Max and I the talk. It was a little different than the one he gave to Willow's dates. Less threatening but more intimidating. Or maybe that was my view on it because he knew I had a thing for his daughter. If Max said she was off limits, I could only imagine James was on the same page.

"Hey, man. Willow's gonna be here in a minute. She doesn't know I'm heading back home today, so give me a few minutes to talk to her will ya?"

"Of course," I agree as I pull a shirt over my head. When he told me Willow was bringing us breakfast, even though I'd just gotten back from her house, my dick got hard. A tent appeared in my loose-fitting shorts, and I thanked my lucky stars Max was on the other side of the island where he couldn't see my physical reaction to the mention of Willow.

One cold shower later and my dick was under control. For now.

Until I heard her voice. Knowing he needed time to talk to her, I locked myself in my bathroom and took care of business, coming with such intensity I bit my bottom lip hard enough I drew blood.

That's what she does to me. The sound of her voice, the smell of the vanilla lotion she rubs all over her body, the mention of her name …

I'm so screwed. Max is going to catch on because I

can't hide the way I feel about her anymore. I don't want to.

FIFTEEN

Willow

Sneaking around is kind of hot. I mean, don't get me wrong, the lying part sucks. I'm terrified we're going to get caught at some point. But the quickies, heated stares, faint brushes of his fingers on my body, whispered promises ... shit, he knows how to rev my engine.

And he takes every opportunity he has to get me going.

Which has been a challenge the last week considering Max has been hanging around more than usual. Watching our every move.

Not that I don't love my brother, but I can still see he's hurting. The pain in his eyes is slowly starting to lift. He's resembling himself more and more every day. Or so I thought. This morning, when I brought over donuts and bagels at his request, I was surprised to find his eyes bloodshot with dark circles under them as if he hadn't slept.

My concern kicked up a notch when I saw his overnight bag packed, sitting by the couch.

"Where are you going?" I ask, popping open the box

of sweet treats, the smell of sugary goodness wafting through the air.

"Home. Evie has prom tomorrow night, and I want to be there to greet the guy who's taking her."

That's code for *threaten* her date.

The same way he did mine even though he knew the guy and we'd been dating for close to a year. Luckily for me, Dad was there to keep Max in check. Not that I think he would have punched my date or anything, but the ferocity in his eyes when he spoke was clear.

"Touch her, you die."

"Sleep with her, I'll bury you alive."

Yeah, needless to say, my boyfriend didn't lay a hand on me. At the time I was pissed. I was finally ready to sleep with him, to give him the gift of my virginity. I didn't want to go off to college without experience. And with one glare, Max ruined my chances.

Turns out, he'd been cheating on me for weeks with some girl from another school. He broke up with me the day after prom and went to her dance the following weekend.

Yeah, he was a real gem. Max may have saved me from a greater heartache, but it doesn't mean I'm going to watch him go balls-to-the-wall on Evie's date. Joe's a nice boy. They're only friends. More like brother and sister. The only reason they're going together is because both of them are single right now and they want to have fun.

"I'm headed over tomorrow morning if you want to ride together. I promised Evie I'd do her hair and makeup."

It's a lie, but one Evie will back me up on as soon as I

talk to her and explain why I had to lie to Max. That it would be in her benefit to go along with it. Plus, I do want to see her in the dress she picked out, all dolled up. And the reaction on Max's face when he realizes his baby sister isn't a baby anymore.

"Nah. Mom said the kitchen sink was leaking and that she couldn't get the lawn mower started the other day, so I have some stuff to get done today." His voice is flat, void of all emotion.

I can tell he's not excited to go back home, to relive the memories. Honestly, neither am I, but it's something we're going to have to get used to because Mom will never sell that house. Even though it's too big for just her, and the maintenance and upkeep are going to be a full-time job for her.

"You know, we should really look into hiring someone to help once Evie's gone. Especially before winter. Someone needs to help her close the pool for the season, and I don't want her trying to shovel the driveway by herself."

"I've already discussed it with Chris. He knows a guy I guess."

Of course he does. Chris Graham, Finn's dad, knows everyone. He owns the largest real estate firm in the area. His connections span far and wide.

"That's great." I feign excitement, but my smile doesn't reach my eyes.

Sliding onto the stool next to me, Max takes a sip of his coffee before closing his eyes and letting out a sigh.

"You look tired, Maxy. Are you sure you don't want to wait until tomorrow? I'll drive up with you."

"No, I'm afraid if I let the leak go too long it'll damage the subfloor. Mom said it wasn't that bad, but she didn't even notice it until the rug in front of the sink was soaking wet, which means it's been leaking for a while now."

"Well, I guess I'm just going to have to go with you today then. Let me call Kendall and rearrange some things." Just as I'm pulling out my phone, Max lays his hand on top of mine and shakes his head. When our eyes meet, his look empty.

"I need to go alone, Lo. I need to think while I drive. To clear my head before I get there. I appreciate the offer and I know you're trying to help but please let me do this."

The pleading in his voice causes my heart to ache in my chest. I know what's on his mind. I wish he'd talk to me. Lean on me. If it weren't for Kendall and Finn, I'd still be where Max is right now. A deep state of depression, sliding further into the darkness every day.

"Talk to me, Max. You need to talk to someone. You can't go on like this, bottling everything up." He shakes his head, averting his eyes to the steaming cup of coffee in his hands. "One thing. Tell me one thing that keeps you up at night, because I can tell you're not sleeping, and I'll drop it. For now."

"Our last conversation was a fight," the words are barely above a whisper as they slip past his lips.

Well, shit. That's not what I expected him to say, but it explains everything about the way he's been acting, how hard it's been for him since Dad died. They barely ever fought but when they did it could get explosive. Both are/were passionate and fought to have their voices and opinions heard. Neither liked to back down, especially when they believed they were right.

"The last time I talked to Dad I accidentally hung up on him because I had my phone pressed between my shoulder and ear," I start, remembering the day like it was yesterday, not weeks ago. "Instead of calling him back, I sent him a text. I could have called him, I wasn't busy, but we weren't talking about anything important, so I sent a text. Don't you think I regret that?"

"I hadn't talked to him in a week, Willow. I was angry."

"About what?"

"He was still pressuring me to take the bar exam."

It's a fight they'd had plenty of times over the years. Max refused to be a lawyer, hated that my dad defended assholes. My father knew Max would make a great attorney and was always encouraging him to change his mind. It wasn't Max's passion, but my father refused to accept it. Max still doesn't know what he wants to do with his life so he's studying international business which my father called a cop out.

"Listen closely because I'm only going to say this once." I turn on my stool to face my brother. When he doesn't look up at me, I place my hands on his cheeks and force him to make eye contact with me. "Dad loved you. You're his son. His firstborn. Pride and joy. No matter what you decide to do with your life, he's going to be proud of you. Did he want you to follow in his footsteps? Yes. He wanted us to take over the firm. He wanted us to carry on his legacy. Do I think you could do that? Of course. You can do whatever you set your mind to. Do I think you would have been happy? Absolutely not.

"I love law. I love studying about cases and reading the history behind how laws came to be. You have no interest in preparing depositions and spending your day in and out of courtrooms. That's fine. He would have gotten it eventually. He would have understood. You want to be a plumber and fix leaky sinks for a living because that's what makes you happy, do it." I feel Finn walk into the room behind me, his unique scent overwhelming my senses, but I don't look over my shoulder.

"All he cared about was your happiness, Max. At the end of the day, as long as you're doing something that puts a smile on your face, something you love and are passionate about, he would be happy for you. Sure, the last words you shared probably weren't nice, but do you think that meant he didn't love you? Because honestly, I'm not sure there's anything in this world you could have done that would have made him love you less. He pushed you to be great because he knew you could. Don't let one conversation destroy the good memories."

Max stares at me with tears freely streaming down his face for what feels like hours before he finally pulls me in for a hug.

"I really needed to hear that, Lo. Thank you."

"It's the truth, big brother. Evie was Dad's little girl. I was his mini-me. But you, you were his favorite. The one who changed his world. You made him a father."

The sound of the toaster popping catches my attention, and when I finally glance behind me, Finn is standing with his back to us. His shoulders are slumped forward as he spreads cream cheese over his bagel.

Releasing Max after a kiss to his cheek, I can see the weight my words have lifted off his shoulders. His eyes are brighter, even though they're still glistening with tears. His smile is small but genuine.

"So," he says, clearing his throat as he reaches for his now empty coffee mug, "what are your plans tonight?"

"Nothing," I reply at the same time Finn says, "Relaxing."

"Okay." Max draws out the word as he looks between Finn's back and my face.

"Want to come home with me, man?"

Finally turning to face us, Finn shakes his head as he takes a giant bite of bagel, his words muffled. "Nah."

"If you don't have any plans, why not? You can help me scare the fuck out of Evie's prom date. I guarantee that's going to be a good time."

Finn chuckles, shoving another bite in his mouth.

"Julian and I might hit the rec center, lift a little. He's already prepping for next season, and I told him I'd work out with him. Most of the other players went home for the summer and he's been bugging me to go so I can spot him."

Odd that he'd use Julian as an alibi considering they *never* hang out alone. Sure, Max and Finn have a rather large group of friends, and when they're together everyone gets along, but that doesn't mean some of them don't mix like oil and water. Julian and Finn are only one example. They respect each other but don't feel the need to hang out.

"I'm surprised you have any energy at all after the late nights and early mornings you've been pulling."

Shit. So, Max has noticed Finn's absence the last few weeks. He's been waiting for him to fall asleep before sneaking over, walking instead of driving so it's not as obvious, and then running home early in the morning to make it look like he has a reason to be coming around sunrise.

Finn said it's been working. Max hasn't done more than nod in his direction. Most of the time, Max is still sound asleep when Finn gets back home. He hasn't asked him any questions, hasn't pushed for why he's suddenly taken an interest in running in the mornings. We figured he didn't care.

"Nah."

I can feel the tension in the room growing exponentially by the second as Finn and Max stare each other down. My eyes flick between the two of them, my heart pounding against my chest.

When Max throws his head back, laughing, I let out a huff of breath in release, sucking it right back in when he speaks. "What's her name?"

Playing it cool, Finn raises his eyebrow but doesn't answer.

"Come on, man. I know there's someone. You've been stomping around here, brooding, all year. Suddenly you're a chipper son of a bitch and you're gonna try and tell me that the sudden change has nothing to do with the fact you're getting laid on the regular?"

My mouth drops open in shock as I slowly turn to look at Finn. He was miserable all year like me. I mean, I know

I was hurting after I woke up and found him gone. I guess I didn't realize he was, too. I didn't give much thought to how he was doing, assuming he was getting along fine since he walked away from me.

"It's just, Lo, man. You can tell me in front of her. Unless ..." His voice trails off, but before either of us can defend ourselves, he finishes his sentence. "Do we know her? Is that why you're keeping it a secret?"

Yes, brother. You could say that. You *do* know her.

Looking at Finn, I try to communicate with my eyes.

What are you waiting for? Say something. Cover our asses. Lie!

"It's just new, that's all."

"I'm happy for you. Honestly, I was worried you wouldn't find someone. Girls hang all over you and you never spare them a glance. Whoever she is, she must be special to have caught your attention."

"Very," is all Finn says before popping the last of his bagel in his mouth, chewing slowly as he stares at me.

Is he trying to make it obvious?

"Bring her to the Memorial Day party. I want to meet this chick," Max says, sliding off his stool. "If she can put a smile like that on your face, I know I'm going to like her."

They share a bro-hug, pat each other on the back, and then Max is out the door. It's barely closed before Finn sweeps me into his arms and carries me down the hall into his room.

"Smooth, Finn. Real smooth. Now he's expecting you to bring a girl to the party with you. A girl that's *not* his little sister," I say as he places me on my feet.

"Looks like we have two weeks to figure out how to break the news to him then," he replies, wrapping his arms around my waist and pulling me tight against his body. "Until then, I can think of a few things we could do to keep this smile on my face."

I bet he can.

SIXTEEN

WILLOW

"Are you sure this is a good idea?" I ask Finn as he merges to get off the highway, sinking deeper into my seat.

"Yes, it's going to be fine. He thinks I'm seeing someone so that actually works in our favor. Just play it cool, okay? He's not going to suspect anything. Not after he called me for help last night."

When Finn says help, he means to vent. Max was under the kitchen sink. He'd taken the plumbing apart, fixed the PVC pipe with a pinhole leak in it, and was attempting to hook everything back up. Let's just say it wasn't going well. I could hear Max screaming into the phone as Finn attempted to calm him down and walk him through the steps he was reading off Google.

"You weren't much help," I state, resting my head against the back of my seat as I turn to look at him.

He's smiling, his eyes focused straight ahead, as he flies down the backroads leading to my house. "And that's why I'm here. How's your mom supposed to wash dishes or cook if she can't use her sink?"

"You said he was going to call a plumber." Not that either of us believed him. Max is a stubborn ass.

Finn chuckles as he takes the last curve leading to our subdivision. It's on the outskirts of town, or at least it used to be. The town is growing, expanding. What used to be a small housing development surrounded by corn fields as far as the eye could see is now the largest subdivision in the county with a strip mall on one side and vacant land on the other.

"Quit trying to push me away, LT. I already told you, I'm not letting you escape this time. You're mine, and the sooner you realize that the better."

Rolling my eyes, I focus out my window for the last leg of our journey, letting his words sink in. Yes, I want to be his. I am his. There never has been or will be another man who will make me feel the way Finn does. That doesn't mean I don't think we shouldn't still play it cautious. Whether Max thinks he's seeing someone else or not.

As we pull into my parents' driveway, I take in the massive two-story house I've always called home. I want to own a home exactly like it someday and fill it with kids the way my parents did. Three to be exact. I want the sounds of water splashing in the pool and laughter to be the music floating on a summer breeze. The smell of the grill wafting through the open windows.

"You ready for this?" Finn asks as he opens his door to get out.

"Yeah, why wouldn't I be?"

"You looked lost for a second. I thought maybe you needed a second."

"Just thinking, that's all." Turning in my seat to exit the vehicle, I feel Finn place his hand on my arm and stop, glancing over my shoulder at him.

"Care to share?"

I'd love to share everything with him. For him to be the father to my children and the one standing in front of the grill, cooking dinner for us.

Of course, that's not what I say. Who would after two weeks? No one. That would scare him off faster than an angry, irate Max when he finds out the dirty, little secret we're keeping from him. "Just thinking, that's all."

He doesn't push me for more, but as soon as we walk through the front door, I wish he had. It would have given us another moment of peace before the utter chaos that was exploding in front of my eyes.

My siblings are having a standoff. Toe to toe. Barely a foot of space between them.

Max is screaming at Evie about her dress.

Evie is shouting about being a—these are her words not mine—*grown ass woman* who didn't ask for his permission.

My mom is attempting to talk over both of them, to get them to cool down. She's waving her hands between their glares, but nothing is shutting them up.

"Well, this is fun," Finn mumbles from behind me.

"You insisted on coming. Welcome to the show." I spread my arms out wide, motioning around the room.

"Want me to cause a distraction?" he offers, sliding up next to me, brushing his fingers over mine.

"What did you have in mind?"

"Well, the way I see it, I can do one of two things. I

can either kiss you or shout that we're banging. Both will get their attention." I feel my face contort in horror at his suggestion. Before I can say a word though, Finn nudges me with his shoulder. "Just smile and play along."

"Finn—"

"Willow and I are sleeping together," he shouts over the yelling match Evie and Max are still engrossed in.

You could have heard a pin drop within a five-block radius. Max slowly pivots to face us, his jaw hanging open in shock. I wait for Finn's announcement to register, for fists to fly, but as each second ticks by, and nothing happens, I let out the breath I was holding and start laughing.

"You should see the look on your face, Maxy. Priceless!"

Finn starts laughing with me, and slowly Evie and Mom join us. Max only shakes his head and walks away. After our laughter fades, and we've said our hellos, I go in search of my brother. I'm not surprised I find him sitting in my father's home office. The rich scent of leather surrounds me as I step inside, memories of all the time I spent in here with him smacking me across the face.

"Someone can't take a joke this afternoon." I plop down next to him on the sofa.

"You two have a twisted sense of humor."

"It got you to stop fighting, didn't it?"

"You couldn't have just said hello, Lo?" he asks, finally turning to face me. I can see the turmoil raging in his eyes. "You and Finn, you guys have a weird friendship. I don't get it. When he said you two were together, I started freaking out."

Well, shit. I expected him to blow a gasket, not stop and think about the words coming out of Finn's mouth. I should be honest with him and tell him the truth. It's the perfect opportunity to confess that what Finn said is fact not fiction, but as much as I've been trying to convince myself he's not ready to hear it, I'm not sure if I'm ready to confess it. Because once the words slip passed my lips, it makes it real.

It means things can fall apart.

That I could lose him.

He could hurt me.

So instead, I do what I do best and deflect, giving him the truth but at the same time keeping my secret.

"Finn's a good guy, Max. He's your best friend for a reason. He cares about me, and I care about him. He protects me when you're not around. He wouldn't hesitate to help me if I asked."

"Do you love him?" he asks without breaking eye contact.

God, I wish I were a better liar.

"I do. He has a big heart. He's the kind of man I want to spend the rest of my life with."

"Why don't you marry the guy then and put him out of his misery?" His words shock me, causing me to suck in a deep breath, my hand flying to my heart. Then he starts laughing. Hard. Holding his stomach as he tips his head back.

I'm still in shock from his little quip, so I smack him in the chest and then rush out the door, his parting words coming out rushed between laughs.

"I was kidding, Willow. Lo, I'm sorry."

Not funny, Max. Because I would marry that man in a heartbeat if he ever asked. No matter how you feel about it.

It's not hard to avoid the guys the rest of the day. Mom, Evie, and I head to my parents' room to help her start getting ready while they attempt to finish fixing the sink. Mom's eyes are glistening with tears as we sit on the bed, waiting for Evie to show us the final result of our hard work.

We curled her long, golden locks before pinning half of them up. I tried to convince her to leave tendrils around her face, but she wasn't having it. My little sister is a lot like Max when it comes to getting her way. She doesn't like to budge. It was hard enough to get her to let me curl her hair. She would have gone with a messy bun on top of her head if I let her.

"You okay?" I ask Mom, taking her hand in mine and giving it a little squeeze.

"I'm fine. Just wishing your dad were here today. He loved watching you guys get dressed up for things like this."

"You mean he enjoyed threatening our dates," I joke, resting my head on her shoulder.

"That too. God, did he love scaring the crap out of those boys. Do you remember Evie's first dance, her freshman year?"

Pink satin gown. Butterfly clips in her hair. More makeup than necessary. She looked like a Barbie doll.

Kendall would have loved that look.

"Yeah, sort of, why?"

"It was the first time in a long time I saw your father

cry. You guys had all left. Your father had threatened both of your dates, but did you know he also threatened Max and Finn? It was hilarious. And then once the house was quiet, we curled up on the couch and he cried. He wasn't ready to let you guys go. He wanted to keep you all little forever, but he knew he couldn't. Evie going to high school broke him."

I can hear the sorrow in her voice as she replays the night over again in her head.

"Why did he threaten Max and Finn?"

"He said they needed to hear it. They were seniors in high school, taller than most father figures, and he wanted to scare them straight, to make sure they knew he expected them to respect their dates the same way he expected boys to respect you girls. It was sweet, actually … funny but sweet."

I try to picture my dad having his you-will-treat-my-daughter-with-respect conversation with Finn.

"When you walked in today and Finn said you two were together, my heart leapt. Your father would have been so happy." Sitting straight up, I stare at my mother in shock. "I mean, not about the way he announced it. That was a bit over the top."

"What do you mean?"

"Your dad always thought you two would end up together. I think that's part of why the boys got that conversation that night. He wanted to make sure Finn heard the speech at least once. Not that he needed to hear it. That boy has always been good to you."

My head is spinning, but before I can ask her anything else, Evie walks out of my bathroom. She spins around so we can get the full effect as the doorbell chimes. Evie's eyes go wide as she starts bouncing up and down.

"Calm down. It's just Joe. Unless there's something you need to tell us before you leave?" I ask, raising my eyebrow at her.

She brushes me off, rolling her eyes dramatically. "Can't a girl just be excited for her last dance of high school?"

"She can, and it appears she is. So, let me be the first to tell you how gorgeous you look," I say, walking over and pulling her into my arms.

Mom wraps her arms around both of us, squeezing tight.

"My beautiful girls," Mom starts, her voice shaking, a clear sign she's already crying. By the time we finally pull apart, there are tears streaming down my face as well.

"We need to get down there before Max scares him off," Evie states, her voice shaking a little at the thought.

"Don't worry. It's under control," I promise her. When she looks at me skeptically, I laugh. "Why do you think Finn is here? If there's anyone that can get Max to shut up and back down, it's him."

Mom laughs as she walks out of the room ahead of us. I'm about to follow her when Evie places her hand on my arm.

"About Finn …" Her voice trails off, and I know what she's asking even though the words don't pass her lips.

"It's not what you think—"

"What do I think?"

"That we're sleeping together like he yelled loud

enough the neighbors probably think we're shagging, too."

"Shagging?"

"Sorry. We watched *Austin Powers* last night."

"You and Finn?"

Well, shit.

"Kendall was there, too," I lie.

"Right, and you're not sleeping together," she huffs with a laugh.

"Evie, this isn't the time or place to have this discussion unless you want your date to leave without you."

Her eyes practically bulge out of her head. "This conversation isn't over," she whispers as she walks past me.

Of course it's not. Because my family is nothing if not invested in my personal life. And I can't seem to keep a secret to save my life. Not that Finn's announcement helped our case.

SEVENTEEN

Finn

SCREAMING THAT WE WERE SLEEPING TOGETHER PROBABLY wasn't the best idea to get Max to shut up, but it worked. I only wish I'd had my camera ready because his face said it all. He was trying to process my announcement; I could see him trying to put the pieces together in his head.

My inability to leave Willow alone, even at their father's funeral. Me, sneaking out and back in. Willow suddenly coming around more. The sexual tension between us.

Shit!

That's not a good idea. I was about to tell him I was joking when Willow came to my rescue. Laughter ensued for everyone but Max. He stormed off in a huff, and I knew I was going to get shit later on. Thankfully, Willow went after him, so I didn't have to deal with his rage right away.

Keep in mind, Max never disappoints.

As soon as the girls disappeared upstairs to help Evie finish getting ready, I found him under the kitchen sink, cursing under his breath as he attempted to fix the plumbing.

"Can I take a look?" I ask, kicking his shoe.

"Knock yourself out," he replies, scooting out from under the sink, handing me the flashlight.

As soon as I'm situated and sure he can't see my face, I feel out his mood.

"So ... not a good idea to scream I'm banging your sister, huh?"

"Can't say I enjoyed that."

"You do realize I'd never announce something like that in front of a girl's family, right? I have more class than that." It's the truth. When Willow and I decide to tell everyone, the words will be delicately chosen. I respect her and her family.

"I swear to God, man. I don't know if I was more shocked at your confession or angry that you touched her."

"I touch her all the time," I laugh, trying to keep the conversation light. Holding out my hand, I call for the wrench. When I feel it land in my hand, it's with more force than I'm prepared for. "Dude, calm down. Willow is a princess, and she deserves to be treated like one. If she were mine, you know I'd take care of her, protect her. Not just physically either. I'd guard her heart. Stop pissing all over her and give her a chance to live a little."

"I'm not pissing all over her. That the stupidest thing I've ever heard."

Sliding out from under the sink, I hand him back the wrench with as much force as he handed it to me, maybe more, drawing his attention. "You scare away any guy who looks in her direction. She doesn't even realize half the shit you've done to keep guys away from her."

"And she doesn't need to know. I'm her brother. It's my duty to protect her."

"Even from me? Because the way I see it, if there's anyone you can trust with her it's me. I'm your best friend, man. You know me better than anyone, and you know I'd never do anything to hurt your sister."

He lets the words sink in, rolling them around in his head like he can't decide if he agrees with me or not. The moment the light bulb clicks, I slide back under the sink so he can't see my reaction. Or the smile on my face while I lie to him.

"Something you want to tell me, *friend*?"

"No, but if there ever were, I'd hope you'd be happy for her. For me. I'm not going to lie to you and say that I don't care about your sister. We both know I do."

"And she cares about you."

Fuck yes, she does. More than he knows.

"What's your point?" I ask as I run my finger across all the lines to make sure they're hooked up correctly. The last thing I want is to get a shower when he turns the water on.

"My point is this—"

"You know what," I interrupt, not wanting to hear what he has to say, "I'm not interested in what you think because if the day ever comes when you sister decides she wants to give me a chance, I'm not going to ask you for permission. I'm going to lay my heart on the table and pray she wants it."

Either I've stunned Max into silence, or he walked

away. When I peek out the doors, his shoes are still visible so I'm assuming the former.

"Turn the water on," I state, hoping he can table the conversation. At least for now. I'm not sure how much more I can handle without adding to the heavy ass bag of lies I feel like we've already told him.

He does, and when it doesn't start raining on me, I slide out from under the sink and stare at my best friend. He's searching my eyes for something. The truth maybe. He doesn't say, though, because the doorbell rings and he suddenly remembers the real reason he came home, a small smirk playing on his lips.

"You got my back?" he asks, shutting the faucet off and kicking the cupboard doors closed.

"Hell yes." Holding my fist out, he bumps his with mine and we take off for the front door, side by side. Poor Joe is going to shit his pants when he sees us because we are a force to be reckoned with. We always have been, and we always will be. No matter what.

Kudos to the kid for not running the other way when we open the door. You can tell he's nervous, his hands shaking as he holds onto the corsage he brought for Evie, but he holds his head high as Max leads him down the hall to his father's office. Being in here brings back memories of the night he gave us *the talk*.

"So, you're taking my little sister to prom?" Max asks as he shuts the door behind us. Before Joe has a chance to answer, he continues, jumping right into his father's speech. I couldn't be prouder at the moment. It's like he memorized it, nailing all the major points, causing a sheen of sweat to break out on Joe's forehead.

Treat her like a lady. Open doors for her, pull out her chair. Basically, be a goddamn gentleman.

Have her home on time. No detours. No driving around. Respect her family.

No touching her inappropriately. This includes her butt, boobs, and *girly area*.

Most importantly, no sex or anything that could lead to it. Clothes must stay on at all times. His and hers.

I'm enjoying the show when Evie bursts through the door, looking like she's going to strangle Max with her bare hands. He hadn't even gotten to the best part yet. What will happen if Joe breaks a rule. Not that he needs to say it, it was implied. I think Joe got the message loud and clear.

I know I did when James gave me the same talk.

EIGHTEEN

Willow

Three drinks in and I'm feeling more relaxed than I have in my brother's presence since last summer when I first slept with Finn. It's by design though. Because Max refused to head back home. He insisted he was waiting for Evie to get home from prom. That's what Dad would have done and that's what he's going to do.

So, the three of us are lounging by the pool, drinking a fruity punch Finn whipped up, reminiscing about high school. The dances. The parties. People we dated. Who's doing who now.

We're gossiping.

Yup. And the boys are leading the conversation like a bunch of little girls, giggling ever few seconds.

Looks like I should have packed an overnight bag. Max planned on staying the night, but I wasn't expecting to be here this late. Finn and I were going to have one last night alone at his place. But neither of us are in any shape to drive back to school, not that Finn would ever let anyone behind the wheel of his precious Sasha. I don't think he's even let Max drive her.

"So, Mom told me a funny story today," I say when their laughter quiets. "Something about you two getting the very lecture Max delivered to Joe earlier from Dad."

Finn and Max share a knowing grin.

"What? Are you going to tell me what he said or not?"

"You've heard him give the speech before," Max says.

"Somehow I feel like him giving it to the two of you was different. Maybe less threatening."

Finn's burst of laughter has me whipping my head in his direction. He's seated on the other side of Max, much to my dismay. I was in the middle lounger, but Max stole my seat when I went to the bathroom.

"Try more threatening," Max blurts out, his own laughter bubbling from his chest.

"What? Why? He knows you two treat women right."

"That's exactly it. He wanted to make sure we didn't forget it either. If I remember right, his exact words were, *'If you look at her and your pants get tight, look away,'* or something like that." Max's words cause my mouth to drop open in shock.

Oh. My. God.

"He definitely said the word dick. Twice, I think, because the way he was looking at me when he said it made mine shrivel up a little," Finn adds through deep breaths, attempting to get control of his laughter.

"He did not!" I exclaim, trying to picture my dad talking about Finn's dick.

"Finn might be right. I do remember having the feeling like I needed to hide my balls after that conversation. Needless to say, sex was the last thing on my mind that night. Heather didn't take the rejection well."

That's because my brother's high school "girlfriend", if you could call her that, was a mega slut. Rejection wasn't something she was familiar with when it came to sex. I'm fairly certain she slept with half of their graduating class and half of mine.

Those messages you find written on the walls of bathroom stalls, that was like Heather's business card.

For a good time, call ...

And the thing is, she wasn't even apologetic about who she was. She didn't care if people thought she was a slut. I will give her some props, though. If she was dating someone, they were the only person she was sleeping with. When she was with Max, he was the only one dipping his stick in her.

For his sake, let's hope he wrapped it up.

"What about you, Finn? Did my dad ruin your chances of getting laid that night, too?"

His face contorts a little before he shakes his head, causing my stomach to churn.

"Hell no!" Max hollers. "Finn went with that college chick. If he didn't put out, he would have ruined his badass rep with the ladies."

It's clear Finn doesn't like this conversation, but Max can't tell because his back is to Finn. So, when he keeps talking, I'm not surprised Finn gets up and walks inside.

"Way to go, jackass," I snarl at him as I stand, grabbing my empty glass off the patio.

"What'd I do?"

"You insulted your best friend."

Looking over his shoulder at where Finn was seated, Max shrugs. "It's the truth. He did sleep with that chick."

"Did you ever think maybe he regretted it? Or at least wasn't proud of it? That talking about it was disrespectful? I know you've slept with a few *ladies* that you'd rather not talk about. Put yourself in his shoes for a second. Would you want him to air all your dirty laundry?"

"You're always defending him," Max says, jumping up and standing close enough I can feel his breath on the tip of my nose. "Is there really something going on between you two, Lo? Because if there is—"

"If there *was*, I'm not obligated to tell you shit, Max. This is my life."

"Are you kidding me? You're seeing my best friend?"

"I didn't say that. I said if I wanted to, I could, and there is nothing you could say or do about it to change the situation."

"That's rich, Willow. You want me to start dating your friends now? Kendall's single, right? We can double date. Have sleepovers. Is that what you want?"

Vivid images of Kendall and Max screaming at each other in the middle of a restaurant bring a smile to my face, and before I can stop myself, I'm laughing. I can't even blame it on the alcohol either.

"This isn't funny!"

"Yes," I huff out. "Yes, it is. Because you and Kendall would kill each other. The sex would probably be hot, a hate fuck for sure, but I doubt you'd make it that far before trying to strangle the life out of each other."

Max groans and turns to walk away but stops when I grab his hand and pull him into a hug. As soon as my laughter subsides, I whisper in his ear.

"I love you, Maxy. You're my big brother, and I know you care about me. You want to protect me from all the ugly in this world and shelter me from heart break. I appreciate it, but I'm a big girl. I can protect myself and make my own decisions."

"Are you dating Finn? Please don't lie to me, Willow. If you two are together, for real, in love, together, together, I have a right to know."

Are we?

Together, together?

We haven't had that conversation. I mean, not exactly. He's said some things and I've agreed with them, but maybe it's time we have a sit-down discussion about what we are. About what we mean to each other.

"Honestly," I start, pulling back but holding him at arm's length, "I don't know. I care about Finn, and he cares about me. We're friends. We hang out and have fun. If we ever decide to be *together together,* as you put it, you'll be the first person I call. But just to be clear, it won't be to ask for permission. And if it ever happens, I expect you to be happy about it because he is your best friend in the world and a decision like that won't be made without serious thought."

Max searches my eyes for the truth. Well, I just gave it to him. Because as soon as Finn and I sit down and hash it all out, I know we're going to have to tell Max.

Not ask, tell him we're together.

What's the saying? *It's better to beg for forgiveness than ask for permission.*

Well, I have no intention of doing either. Because I'm

not sorry about the way I feel about Finn, and I have a feeling he's not sorry either.

"I can't believe you basically told him we were together," Finn confesses as he walks me up to my apartment.

The entire drive home I was trying to find a way to prepare Finn for how Max might react when he gets home today. When the tall buildings of downtown finally came into view, the words spilled out. Not as eloquently as I would have liked either. It was more like word vomit as I rushed to warn him about the conversation Max and I had last night.

"You basically did the same. Maybe it's a good thing. At least it won't come as a complete shock when we tell him now."

"So, you think we should come clean?" he probes as I open the door to my apartment only to be greeted with Kendall's naked backside.

"Holy shit!" I holler before pushing Finn back into the hall and slamming the door behind us.

I can hear Kendall on the other side of the door, shouting orders at someone, cursing at herself.

"That looked an awful lot like—"

"Don't say it. I know exactly what was going on in there."

"But that was—"

"I don't care who it was, and honestly, I don't want to know. That's a visual image I'll never be able to erase."

My phone buzzes in my purse. When I pull it out, I find a text from Kendall apologizing and giving me the all clear to come inside. Hesitant, I slowly open the door, peeking my head inside to find the living room empty.

Finn follows me straight into my bedroom where I close and lock the door behind us and text Kendall back.

ME: Didn't mean to interrupt. We're in my room if your friend wants to leave. Or whatever. He can stay.
K: He's going to leave. Things are awkward now.
ME: Okay. Just let me know when he's gone, and we can talk.
K: I never want to talk about this ever again. Ever.

Me either, girl. Me either.

Finn wraps his arms around me from behind as I plug my phone in to charge. I turned it off last night before I went to bed, so it didn't die since I was unprepared to stay at my mom's. Not that I was able to sleep after my conversation with Max. I was hoping Finn would slip into my room and hold me, but he didn't.

"I need a nap," I confess.

"Me, too. I slept like crap. I'm too tall to sleep on that couch."

"I was expecting you to crawl in with me last night. What happened?"

"I wasn't about to disrespect your parents' house. Plus, your brother was asleep on the other couch. If he woke up and I was gone, how would I have explained that?"

Good point.

Finn tugs me toward my bed, pulls back the covers, and we both crawl in fully clothed after kicking off our shoes. Tucking me against his body, Finn kisses my cheek and is asleep in a matter of minutes, snoring lightly in my ear. It doesn't take me long to follow his lead, his warm embrace and the steady rise and fall of his chest making me feel safe.

My phone ringing wakes me with a start. The first thing I notice is that Finn is no longer in bed with me. The second, it's still light outside, meaning he couldn't have left that long ago.

"Hello?" I answer, not bothering to look at who's calling.

"Have you seen Finn?" Max asks.

Looking at the time, I notice we've only been back in town for about two hours.

"He dropped me off a little while ago. Why?"

"I just got home and he's not here. Wait." There's a long pause, and then Max says, "Never mind. He just walked in the door."

"Okay. You boys have fun. I'm going to go back to my nap."

"Why are you sleeping? It's the middle of the afternoon."

"Because I didn't sleep well last night," I counter, laying my head back on my pillow only to be poked in the ear by something. When I turn my head, I find a folded piece of lined paper.

"What kept you up?" Max asks.

"Nothing, I just think I drank that special amount where I was still wired. Not quite drunk but not sober, ya know?"

"Yeah, I get that. I didn't sleep that great last night either."

Good thing Finn was smart enough not to sneak into my room then. Max would have surely caught us.

"You're just pissed Evie made curfew and looked just as beautiful walking in the door as she did out. I know you were looking for a reason to yell at Joe."

Max chuckles, not admitting what we both know as truth, before letting me go. As soon as I hang up, I unfold the paper and sigh.

LT,

Didn't want you to think I was running away so I wrote you this note. I smell bad. Need a shower. Headed home before your brother grows even more suspicious. Let's grab coffee tomorrow and talk more.

Love,

Finn

My heart swells in my chest as I hold the note to my lips. He's so sweet. He knew I would freak out if he wasn't here when I woke up.

There's a knock on my door before I can even close my eyes again. When I call out for Kendall to come in, she peeks her head in the small opening, a grimace on her face.

"Can we talk?"

"Do you want to talk about it?" I counter, patting the mattress next to me.

"Not really," she confesses as she lays down in Finn's spot.

Finn's spot. I like the sound of that. I almost don't want to let her use *his* pillow, so she doesn't ruin the way it smells.

"We're not a serious thing. Not like you and Finn."

"K, you're allowed to sleep with whoever you want. I don't care who he is as long as he makes you happy and treats you good."

"You didn't see his face?" she asks, bolting upright.

"No," I say, stretching out the word far longer than necessary. "Do I want to know?"

Kendall shakes her head. "Not yet. Let me figure this out first. Like I said, we're not serious or anything. Plus, he swears Finn saw his face, so it's not like it's a secret anyway."

"Well, I don't plan on asking Finn, so until you're ready to tell me, your secret is safe. I'll make sure he keeps his mouth shut, too."

"Just stick your boobs in his face. He won't have much to say then, will he?" she jokes, her face breaking out in one of her signature smiles.

There's my best friend.

NINETEEN

Finn

You have to be fucking kidding me!

I did not just walk in on my brother fucking Willow's roommate. He's not that stupid. Last I knew he had a girlfriend, though he wasn't into her as much as she was him.

But of all people ...

I'm going to kill him. He knows better than to screw around with people I care about. I didn't even realize they knew each other that well. Or maybe, that's what the draw was. But he knows Willow, which also means he knew whose apartment he was in. It's not a secret Kendall is her roommate, and by sleeping with her he's putting Willow in an awkward situation if shit doesn't work out.

My thoughts stop me in my tracks when I realize I'm Max in this scenario.

Damn it!

When Willow didn't push to find out who the mystery guy was, I let it go. If they're not serious, if this is just a one-off, she never has to know. If she asks, I won't lie to her, but I'm hoping Kendall will tell her before then. They don't keep many secrets from each other, hence why she's the only person who knows about us, but then again, my brothers and I don't keep secrets either.

They both ran to me the night they lost their virginity and wanted to talk about it.

When Declan thought he knocked his girlfriend up in high school, I was the one he turned to. Thankfully, she was only after attention.

When Micah got drunk at a party his senior year, he called me instead of my parents to come get him. He knew I'd drive two hours home to pick his ass up and cover for him, so he didn't get grounded.

We're close, to say the least. Like Max and his sisters, there's not a lot of years between us. We fought as kids but grew out of that stage when we realized we needed each other more as friends.

As I'm leaving Willows later that afternoon, I shoot him a text. I'm shifting my car into drive when he replies. Knowing I need to get this over with, I put it back in park and grip my phone so I don't throw it.

ME: What the actual fuck, man?
BROTHER: Calm down, old man. You'll give yourself a heart attack. We didn't even have sex.

I want to strangle him for the nickname alone. Why is he trying to piss me off even more than he already has?

ME: Could have fooled me.
BROTHER: She still had her panties on.
ME: Please tell me you aren't fucking her for fun.
BROTHER: And if I am?

ME: I might kill you just for shits and giggles.
BROTHER: Did you just say shits and giggles?
ME: I'm serious. What's going on with you two? When did this even start? How?
BROTHER: That's between me and K. She's a big girl. If she wants to have a little fun that's up to her and I'm happy to see to her needs.
ME: I swear to God if you break her heart, I will sick Willow on you.
BROTHER: Speaking of Willow …

Fuck my life.

ME: Don't try and change the subject.
BROTHER: Just pointing out that you two were behind closed doors when I left. Maybe I'm not the only one who needs to go to confession.
ME: A secret for a secret?
BROTHER: Now you're talking my language. You two finally together?
ME: Something like that. Max doesn't know, and I'd appreciate it if you kept your big mouth shut.
BROTHER: As long as you keep what you saw to yourself, we have a deal.
ME: Wrap it up, little brother. The last thing you need is a baby right now. You can't even take care of yourself.
BROTHER: Oh, it was wrapped. What a waste of a condom.
ME: We'll talk more when I see you next. Until then, stay away from Kendall unless you plan on being more

than a passing fling. Got it?
BROTHER: Yeah, yeah. Thanks, dad.

Max is waiting for me when I walk in the door. I can tell he wants to talk so I do the one thing I promised my brother I wouldn't do; I spill his secret to take the spotlight off of me. I didn't mention his name, just what Willow and I walked in on. It brings a smile to Max's face, and for the first time in weeks, I hear his laugh.

"God, I can practically see the expression on Lo's face," he says as his laughter fades. "I needed a good laugh."

"It's one of those, 'if you were there, it wasn't funny, but if you hear about it, it is' kind of jokes. Because let me tell you, there was nothing funny when she opened that door. Even I cringed."

"Did you get a look at the guy?"

"Yeah," I say, hanging my head. "I want to tell you who it was, but I don't think it's anything serious so I'm not gonna say."

"Doesn't surprise me. Kendall doesn't seem like the relationship kind of girl. It's the one thing her and her sister have in common."

"Kora?"

"Yeah. That girl is wild. The man who finally nails her down is gonna have to be a strong SOB to be able to handle her. I can't spend more than two minutes in the room with her. She's worse than Kendall. Always fucking grating on my nerves." His eyes blaze with something I can't quite put my finger on, but he changes the subject before I can dig deeper. "Got a favor to ask."

"What's up?"

"I'm starting to fix up the frat house this week. I could really use an extra set of hands. Someone who knows what they're doing and can show the guys a few things. It's mainly drywall and painting. There are a few other things but those are the big ones. Think you can give me a hand?"

"Sure." I don't mind helping piece the house back together. Last time I was there it shocked me how far they let it go. The president Max took over for was a real piece of shit. All he cared about was having parties and collecting dues. I know the last few years of leadership have given the Kappa house a bad name. Pledges are afraid to commit to them. Members are left. This is Max's opportunity to fix everything that's broken—the perception of Kappa as well as all the physical pieces of the house that need attention.

"Cool. We're going to start tomorrow morning. I already ordered a bunch of shit that's going to be delivered today. Not a lot of guys stuck around this summer, so I appreciate the extra set of hands and the expertise."

"I worked one summer in construction, same as you. I'm far from being an expert."

It was a fun summer, though. We were outside all day, building houses, using our hands to create a place someone would eventually call home. It was rewarding. And I learned a shit ton. Apparently, I have a knack for fixing things. I actually considered looking for a part-time gig this summer, but I've been a little preoccupied.

TWENTY

Willow

It's close to two o'clock in the morning before Finn arrives. I was about ready to give up on him when my phone alerted me to a text letting me know he was out in the hall. After tiptoeing through the apartment so I don't wake Kendall, I let him in. He silently follows me to my room, and without a word, we crawl into bed, cuddling in the middle. His front to my back. His arm resting over my hip. My head tucked perfectly beneath his chin.

But I can't sleep. There's so much I want to say. We need to talk, and if I don't get this off my chest, I won't be able to sleep tonight at all. So, I'm laying here awake, staring at the wall in front of me, thinking about everything that has changed over the last few weeks. I lost my dad. My heart broke into a million pieces. Then I fell in bed with Finn and slowly my heart has started to heal.

Is it all just sex, though? Does he really mean all the sweet things he whispers in my ear?

He must sense my turmoil because he turns me to face him, tilting my chin so I'm forced to look him in the eye.

"What's the matter, little tree?" His voice is laced with concern, his eyes searching mine.

"Nothing."

Why am I lying to him? We need to have this talk. I need to know where we stand. Staring the conversation is hard, though.

"I'm not buying it, so spill."

"What are we?" It takes me five minutes to work up the nerve to ask him, and all I got out were three little words. Not even the hardest three words I'll ever say to him, either.

"What do you mean?"

"This. Are we just having fun or is it something more?"

"This is everything," he states firmly, his voice leaving no room for negotiation on the subject.

"What does that even mean?" I ask, getting frustrated. Pushing out of his embrace, I sit up and turn away from him. Even though he can't see the tears in my eyes, I close them and take a deep breath, hoping to hold them at bay for a little while longer. "I'm not opposed to hooking up, Finn, but I need to know if that's all this is. I don't want to get my hopes up only to have my heart broken. I just lost my dad. It feels like I'm barely holding on as it is some days."

The bed shifts, and then I hear the heaviness of his footsteps as he moves around the room. There's a dip in the bed in front of me, and when I open my eyes, Finn's there with a smile on his face.

"What's so funny?"

"You are."

"I don't think this is funny at all. I'm serious. I need to know what you want from me." Crossing my arms over my chest, I let out a huff of irritation.

"It's a long list, LT. A very, very long list," he says, his voice taking on a sultry tone. The same tone he uses when he wants to strip me down and take me hard.

"Finn," I plead with him.

"You know what this is. You know how I feel about you. I've shown you with my actions, with my body. If you want me to say the words I will. I have no problem with that, but I'm not sure you're ready to hear them."

"I need the words."

"Okay." Reaching for my hand, he pulls me to stand in front of him. We're both fully clothed, but the moment his hand slides against mine I wish we weren't. "You, Willow Grace Palmer, are everything to me. You're my best friend—don't tell your brother—and the only person I want to fall asleep with in my arms and listen to snore. The one person I want to kiss as soon as I wake up, morning breath be damned. Your smile lights up my world when you walk in a room. Your voice makes me hard even when you're bitching about nothing." That earns him a smack against his chest, but he doesn't falter. "Your heart makes me a believer in something more, something bigger than I've ever felt before. But it's your eyes that seal the deal for me. They're the key to your soul. And when I look into them, I see myself standing next to you. You're mine, Willow, and I'm yours."

I know my mouth fell open at some point in time because when Finn leans in to kiss me, his tongue slips between my lips without needing an invitation. His kiss is just as poetic as his words, and I can feel every ounce of love he has for me.

When he pulls back, he smirks at me. "Is that what you wanted to hear?"

"Good enough." I shrug my shoulders at him as if his words had no effect on me.

"You're going to pay for that, you know," he threatens, lifting me by my hips and tossing me on the bed, covering my body with his before I can scramble away.

"I want to tell you how much I like you, Willow. I want to say those three little words that will change everything but we're not there yet. Just know, that's how I feel, and when the moment's right … one where we're not in your bed, sneaking around, I won't hesitate to say them."

"And I won't hesitate to reply," I say, pulling his lips to mine, effectively ending our conversation.

Finn doesn't seem to mind as he quickly removes first his clothes, tossing them wildly around the room, and then mine.

I can wait a little longer to hear him tell me he loves me because if I'd been paying better attention these last few weeks, years maybe, I would have already known. This conversation wouldn't have been necessary. Still, it makes me feel better about deceiving Max.

We're not a fling. We're not screwing around. This is the real deal.

"Memorial Day?" Finn asks as he sits on the edge of my bed. He was supposed to leave fifteen minutes ago. Max should be waking up any minute and they have a big day planned. Max is officially the President of the Kappa house now and he wants to start making changes right away. Cleaning up the place.

Finn isn't a member of Kappa Omega Lambda, but he was recruited for his muscle and skills. At least, that's the way Finn explained it when he said we wouldn't be able to hang out today. I was hoping with Max, and most of our other friends, occupied we could go to the movies or something without having to worry about getting caught.

I also wanted to talk strategy. After my conversation with Max over the weekend, I've realized we can't keep lying to him. I don't like it. I'm not ready to hire someone to skywrite Finn and I are dating yet, but Max deserves to know. Even if he's not going to like the idea. And what better place to tell him than a party?

"Think about it. Most of our friends will be there. Both of our families. We can tell them all at once and he will be less likely to make a scene in front of everyone."

Averting his eyes, Finn slips into his running shoes and stands. When he turns to face me, I'm surprised to find he's not smiling at me. Instead, he looks worried.

"That's two weeks away, LT. Don't you think we've already been lying to him long enough? We're going to get caught and shit's going to hit the fan. It's already hard enough to ignore you when he's around. My eyes seek you out. My body reacts."

"Stop thinking about me naked when he's around then," I joke, throwing back the thin sheet covering my naked body and kneeling on the bed in front of him. I'm rewarded with one of Finn's signature grins that cause my heart to skip a beat.

That look was only for me.

Stepping to the edge of the bed, he slowly runs his hands up and down my arms, igniting a fire inside of me. I want to pull him back into bed and keep him here all day. Screw going to the movie. We can cuddle, watch a movie here, and stay naked.

"Stop trying to distract me." You can hear the pleading in his voice as he continues to lightly graze my skin, moving from my arms to the curve of my neck and finally to my face, cupping my cheeks. "So tempting."

"You could always stay. Tell Max your girlfriend has you tied to her bed and won't let you leave."

Girlfriend. I really like the way that sounds.

I made him repeat it multiple times last night as he ravished my body twice before we both passed out, completely sated.

Leaning in close, he kisses my lips gently before stepping out of my reach, knowing I was going to pull him in for more.

"Two weeks. If you want to tell him at the party, that's fine. I'll try my best not to fuck you against my bedroom wall while he's in the apartment."

"You would never!"

"I've thought about it more than once."

"Finn!"

"Shhh. Kendall is still asleep. Unless she has company?" He lifts his eyebrow in question, but I shake my head, letting him know she's alone.

"I think it was a fling. She doesn't want anyone to know so don't say anything," I explain.

"I want to know when it started. He never said anything to me." I can hear the irritation in Finn's voice. I want to ask why he cares so much, but then again, I don't. Because if I do ...

"Don't tell me who it is." The words are rushed as I stick my fingers in my ears.

"You still don't know?"

"Didn't see his face, and she didn't want to tell me. I think you're the only person who knows besides them."

Finn scrubs his face with his hands and lets out a huff.

"I don't like it."

"Your opinion doesn't matter. It's not our business."

"But it is my business, and I don't like them together."

"Not your decision. People aren't necessarily going to like us together. That's not going to stop us from moving forward, is it?"

"Hell no."

"Keep that in mind then. Plus, if it really was just a fling, it's probably over now. She was mortified we walked in on her."

"Yeah, I guess so." He pauses, but I can tell there's more he wants to say. "I should probably get going."

Hopping off the bed, I grab my robe and slip my arms through, tying it tightly around my waist. "Let's go, *boyfriend*."

Finn chuckles but leads the way through the apartment, our fingers laced together. After a swift kiss goodbye, he's bounding down the stairs on his way back to his place.

Two weeks and then all the lying and sneaking around will be over. Our relationship will be out in the open. If Max has an issue with it, he's going to have to get over it because I love that man and I want to be able to tell him without the fear of someone overhearing.

"Morning," Kendall groans as she walks into the kitchen. I'm standing in front of the coffee maker, waiting for my cup to finish percolating. They say these single serve machines are faster, but in reality, if you drink more than two cups, they only slow the process down.

"Hey. You okay?" I ask, finally turning around and taking a good look at her.

"Fine." But she's not and anyone with two eyes and a brain can tell.

"Well, you look like shit, so I guess fine is an overstatement." K glares at me but doesn't respond. "Are you sure you don't want to talk about it?"

"Give me your coffee and I'll consider it," she challenges.

Under normal circumstances, it's every woman for herself when it comes to coffee. One look at my bestie and I know whatever is going on with her should not be filed under normal. I've never seen her this exhausted, and I have a feeling it's not from lack of sleep.

Fixing my, now Kendall's, cup of coffee, I hand it over and pop in a fresh pod. We stare at each other as we wait for my cup to brew. Once we both have a coffee in hand, we head into the living room and settle on the sofa.

"Talk, girl. I'm here to listen. No judgment."

Kendall let's out a heavy high but doesn't start talking right away, instead sipping her coffee until its half gone. I don't push her. If it's this hard for her to talk about it, I have a feeling it's more serious than I anticipated. Not just a fling. At least not on her end. Her words only confirm my suspicions.

"I like him."

"Okay. I'm going to assume you mean the guy you were riding on the couch yesterday."

"Yeah. Did Finn tell you who he is?"

"Nope. I swore him to secrecy. I don't want to know unless you want me to."

"Not yet. I don't think it's going anywhere but I do know I like him. We've only hung out a few times. That was the first time we did anything more than kiss. You just happened to walk in right as things were getting hot and heavy."

"Sorry for ruining the party," I joke, hoping to at least get her to smile.

"No, it was perfect timing. He'd just put the condom on, and we were about to, but I'm glad we didn't. I don't think it's going to work out. He's just too … too much. I don't know how to explain it."

Hard to believe, but if it's true, I think it's a clear sign Kendall may have met her match.

TWENTY-ONE

Finn

Colton and Kane are getting on my last nerve. Between taking breaks every five minutes and their bitching, I'm not impressed. Yes, hanging drywall is hard work. It's exhausting. The shit is heavy, and it takes time if you want it done right.

"Y'all know I can leave anytime I want, right? This isn't my house. I don't have to be here," I state when they come back from their fifth break of the day. The only reason I knew they left the room was because of the silence.

These guys aren't lazy. I know this. I've hung out with them before. They're cool as fuck. Colton is a talented musician. His band, Fallen Angels, plays every party the frat hosts. He wants to make a living off his music someday, but his parents are making him get his degree first or they'll cut him off financially.

His roommate, Kane, is smart as hell. The dude can do anything on a computer you need him to. He designed the logo and branding for Colton's band, going as far as having custom guitar picks made. His creative genius blows me away.

And they're both tall, strong guys. They can handle drywall; they just don't want to.

"Come on, man. We need you here," Kane says, turning the air compressor back on as he pushes his sunglasses back up his nose.

Yes, we're inside. Yes, he's wearing sunglasses. He always has them on for some reason.

"Yeah," Colton yells over the hiss. "Can't do this without you."

"And I only have two hands, so get your asses back to work and stop disappearing on me," I state firmly as I lift the drywall board into place while Kane secures it to the wall.

We work in silence for the next hour. Colton cutting the pieces to size while Kane and I get them hung. After both walls are complete, taped, and mudded, I stand back and inspect our work. It's clean. Once the mud is dry and sanded, we can paint. That'll take a few hours, so I decide to pack up my shit and get out of there before Max puts me to work doing something else.

Honestly, I'm happy to help. It gives me something to do during the day, but I didn't realize how long this project was going to take. When Max said only a few guys stayed for the summer, I figured he meant six or seven.

Nope. Only Kane, Colton, and Julian.

Brady showed up yesterday for a little bit to help but he has an internship this summer at some clinic. Julian works every day at a restaurant, sometimes up to twelve hours, so he's not always available. Which leaves the four of us.

If Max hopes to get everything on his wish list accomplished, it's going to take us weeks. Hell, it took two days to do drywall when it should have taken one afternoon.

"You out of here?" I hear Max ask.

"Yeah. I'll be back tomorrow morning. If you can get Tweedledee and Tweedledum to sand the drywall later tonight that would help. We can start painting as soon as you pick out a color."

"Gotta rip up the carpet first."

"Since when?"

"Since I smelled it. I was going to clean it, but I don't think it's salvageable. Too many parties, too much puke. The room will be off limits once it's done."

"What were people doing in your meeting room anyway?"

As little as I know about fraternity life, I do know one thing—every house has a sanctuary, a room no one but members are supposed to be allowed in. That room at the Kappa house looked like every party had been thrown in it for years. It should have been the best-looking room in the place but instead it was the worst.

"That's the thing. It's the one room in the house that should have always been locked yet was the most fucked up one in the place," he says, echoing my thoughts, as he blows out a breath in frustration. "It's like Matt had no fucks left to give. I don't even know where the key is. I have to replace the lock."

Shaking my head, I don't even know what to say. Matt was a douche and he let the house go to shit only for Max to have to bring it back to life. One look at this place and I would turn around and walk away if I were trying to pledge a fraternity. Appearances are everything, and the way this place presents itself is anything but good.

"Let me know what color paint and I'll snag it on my way over along with a lock for the door."

"Thanks for everything, Finn. I really appreciate it. We'll make you an honorary member for life," he jokes.

As much as I love Max and a few of the guys in his frat, he knows I have no interest in being a part of that life. It's not for me. Honorary or otherwise.

"Thanks, but I'll pass. Text me later. I'm gonna shower and grab some food. You headed home soon?"

Not that I care. I just need to know how to plan the rest of my night. Can I head straight to Willow's, or do I need to wait for Max to crash? Because waiting up every night and sneaking out is getting annoying.

Less than two weeks.

I can't wait for this to be over. As much of a rush as sneaking around was when we first started, I'm looking forward to being able to walk out the front door at a decent hour without feeling guilty. I want to be able to take her out to dinner. To walk into a party with her on my arm. To kiss her whenever I want to without caring who's in the room or if someone might see us.

"It'll be later. Don't let that stop you from seeing your girl, though." Max winks at me as he walks off, chuckling to himself.

Bastard. I'm starting to think he's on to us and making me sweat. His comments about me seeing someone are happening more frequently, not that I'm shutting him down. I want him to think I'm seeing someone and pretty soon he'll know exactly who that someone is.

Let him see how happy I am. How happy she makes me.

Maybe it'll lessen the blow if he hasn't figured it out already.

Or maybe he's just fucking with me until I come clean, to see how long I plan to lie to him.

I can't get a good read on him and that scares me more than anything else. Especially since I see him every day, here and at home. Because if I'm not with Willow, I'm with Max. One or the other, not very often both. It's too hard.

To keep my hands to myself.

To not look in her direction and see my future flash before my eyes.

The two-story house with gray shutters. Her in our gourmet kitchen, barefoot, helping me cook dinner. Her belly round with my child. Us in bed together at night, her wrapped in my arms. Waking up next to her and kissing her because I can't get enough of her lips.

My heart beats for hers. I can't wait to announce it to the world.

TWENTY-TWO

WILLOW

ONE WEEK DOWN, ONE TO GO. FINN'S BEEN STAYING HERE most nights and even bought himself a new toothbrush to keep here. Max, busy with fixing all the issues he was 'gifted' from the last president of his fraternity, has been practically living at the frat house. Finn's been spending most of his days helping him get shit in order. The physical labor has drained him, and I know he's ready for Max's tirade to come to an end.

Even Julian was complaining to Finn via text last night. For him to reach out to Finn for any reason is unusual. But to complain about Max means it must be bad.

Apparently, they threw some crazy parties this past year and the house took a beating for it. They've replaced drywall and painted in most of the main areas of the house. Replaced both toilets in the downstairs bathrooms and the carpet in the den. This week's agenda consists of replacing parts of the deck and staining it along with yard maintenance. After that, Finn says it'll only be little things they can do over the summer months.

Buying new furniture. Having someone fix the felt on the pool table.

I get why Max wants the house to look nice. It's a direct reflection of who he is and the fraternity as a whole. Rush week was bad last year, only six pledges in the entire class compared to when Max rushed there was more than double that. He wants to make our dad proud, but also, he wants to leave behind his own legacy when he graduates next year.

And he will. Max will be an active president. He'll make sure the pledges are treated fairly and feel welcome. He's bringing back the big brother program and leading the charge. I'm proud of him, but I also think he's going a million miles a minute to keep from dealing with what's really on his mind.

I should know. I've been avoiding him, so I don't have to deal with what's on mine.

Him finding out about my relationship with Finn.

On the bright side, Kendall's mood seems to be picking up. She was really excited to start her summer job as a camp counselor this morning. I've never seen her so pumped at eight in the morning before. She bounced out of her bedroom, almost running into Finn as he was leaving, made both of us a cup of coffee, even though I was planning on going back to bed, and did the dishes before she left for her orientation.

I cleaned the bathroom and then took a long soak in the tub. I was so caught up reading on my phone the water was ice cold, my toes wrinkled, by the time I finally stepped out. My phone chimes as I'm pulling my T-shirt over my head. I know Finn and Kendall are busy still, so I'm a little surprised.

ALEXIS: Are we still on for Movie Monday?
ME: Hell yes!

Piper and Alexis had to cancel last week. Both of them had tests to study for. Not that I minded. Finn kept me company.

ALEXIS: Good. I need a break. My eyes are starting to cross from all the reading.
ME: Feel free to come over whenever you get out of class. I'm cleaning the apartment a little and doing laundry, so I'll be home.
ALEXIS: If I bring tequila can I do some laundry, too?
ME: Of course.
ALEXIS: You might see me sooner than you think. Piper will be back from class in an hour.
ME: Sounds good. See you then.

I'm not sure how they do it. I need my summers to relax. The last thing I want to do is stress myself out with classes. I was going to take two this summer just so I could have a lighter load in the fall but I'm so glad I dropped them. Unfortunately, that means I have a lot of spare time on my hands. I didn't want to get a job because I wasn't sure how much time I'd be able to dedicate to it but now I'm starting to wonder if it might be beneficial to look for something. Even part time.

The extra cash would be nice, that's for sure. My

savings account isn't growing, and even though I know I have enough to get me through until I graduate, a little buffer wouldn't hurt. Plus, it would give me something to do with my days.

Alexis and Piper walk in the door, each carrying a basket of laundry, shortly before Kendall. Alexis brought the tequila, Piper brought the fixings for nachos, and I had Kendall stop for strawberry margarita mix on her way home. It's going to be a Mexi-inspired movie night.

Nachos, margaritas, and *Selena* because who doesn't love to try and dance like J-Lo in that movie? She's amazing.

Which is exactly what we do. The coffee table is pushed against the wall and all four of us, margaritas in hand, shake our hips, dancing and singing. It's a good thing no one is around to see it because none of us are that coordinated. Piper can carry a tune, Alexis has a few nice moves, and Kendall can make anything look good, but me? I look like an inflatable doll, flailing around. Arms stiff, body lurching.

Slow dancing, sure I can handle that. Moving my body, gyrating to a beat … nope.

Which is why I don't try. Because who wants to embarrass themselves on purpose? Not this girl. Even if I have fun when I attempt to dance. Even if I feel free as I throw my hands in the air and swing my hips.

"Your phone," Kendall says, tossing it to me.

Unprepared, with one hand wrapped around my margarita glass, I juggle it before falls to the ground at Piper's feet. She picks it up and hands it over, but not before looking down at my screen that is lit up with an incoming call.

"Um, Lo?" she asks.

When I see who's calling, I chastise myself for not paying more attention to the time. He said he would call when he got here. Between cooking and dancing, the time got away from me. If I'd known it was this late, I would have made it a point to shoot him a text, let him know not to make the trek over just yet.

"I'll explain later." I take my phone and rush into my room, answering as I close my door behind me. "Hey."

"I'd ask if you're having fun, but I can hear the music and laughter from downstairs," Finn says, a hint of laughter in his voice.

"Movie night." It's not really an answer but it's all I say as I sit down on the edge of my bed, taking a sip of margarita as I will my heart to slow its frantic beating. Piper won't say anything, I know this, but still, I feel a small panic attack coming on.

Our secret is out there. Someone else knows. The chances of other people finding out before we're ready are now greater.

The chance of Max hearing it through our little grapevine of friends if Piper does say something—

"Piper and Alexis?" he asks when I don't offer more of an explanation, lost in my head.

"Yup."

"Want me to come back later?"

I want nothing more than to feel his warm embrace. For him to wrap his arms around me and calm the thunderous roar of my heart. Knowing it's close to midnight already, I contemplate what I want versus what is right. The girls will more than likely be leaving soon. I'm sure they called an Uber to take them back to the dorm. They both have class tomorrow, and as easy as it would be for them to just stay over and get up early, I know they won't. They never do.

"I don't know," I reply honestly as I set my margarita on my bedside table. "I want you here, but I also know the girls won't leave for a little bit and you shouldn't have to wait in the hall."

"So ... I can't come in?"

He could. I mean, if Piper hadn't seen he was calling me, neither of them would have given his presence a second thought. But now ...

"I'm not ready to tell them yet," I confess.

Why? I have no idea.

This is real, I remind myself. Nothing is going to change how you feel about each other.

"Okay," he replies, not an ounce of remorse in his voice. "I'll be at the frat house with your brother all day tomorrow if you want to swing by. I know he's been asking for you to come over. He wants a girl's opinion on a few things and doesn't trust anyone else. You should take him up on it, and if the opportunity presents itself, maybe I can take you somewhere quiet while he's not paying attention."

The idea causes a shiver to run up my spine. Sneaking around right under Max's nose. Where we could get caught at any second, by him or one of his frat brothers. It's hot but also risky. With only a week left before we confess our sins in front of all our friends, it's probably a better idea if we lay low.

"I'll think about it," I retort, refusing to accept or deny his proposal.

"I know I will," he groans. "Sweet dreams, LT."

And then he's gone, hanging up before I can reply because he knows what he just did to me. He turned me on with only his words. He's not even in the room and I crave his touch. His lips. His body wrapped around mine.

He's both my sinner and savior.

And I love it.

Him.

When I rejoin my friends in the living room the credits are playing on the TV as they shimmy their hips to the music, picking up the mess we made. Without a word, I join them, dragging the coffee table in front of the couch. By the time there's no remnants of our antics, Piper and Alexis are rushing out the door, laundry baskets in hand, to meet their waiting Uber driver.

"That was so much fun." Kendall smiles as she drops onto the couch next to me with a plop. "I miss living next door to those girls. We always had a great time."

"Me too. Freshman year was so much fun. I hated the dorms, and I'm glad we got our own place, but I'm so glad we met each other and Piper and Alexis. I can't imagine living with anyone else besides the three of you."

"You sure about that?" I know what she's asking, and a blush creeps up on my face, her only answer. "You could have invited him in, you know. They won't say anything if you ask them not to."

"Yeah, but I'm not ready. Plus, Max deserves to know before I start telling everyone else."

"You better get ready, then. Everyone's going to be at the party next Monday when you two come out of the closet."

"You act like this has been going on forever when it's only been a few weeks."

"Please, Willow. You two have been dancing around each other since I've known you. Probably longer. But especially since last summer. When we stopped hanging out with your brother this year, I just thought you were over it. The parties. The craziness. His frat brothers. But mainly, I figured you wanted to move on from Finn.

"I never would have guessed you were heart broken. Not in a million years, because you never let it show. You pushed on, kept your focus on school, and pretended like he didn't exist. I should have known better, figured it out sooner. But now that you have him, don't be afraid to let your emotions show. Let people see how much you love him. There's nothing to be ashamed about. That boy is crazy about you."

As Kendall's words sink in, I try to remember a time when I wasn't head over heels for Finn. He's the only man I've ever really wanted. Sure, I dated a few people in high school, but none of them were serious. They were nothing more than a passing fling. My heart wasn't available to them. I kept it locked away, waiting for the one man I wanted to gift it to, to open his eyes. I was convinced he didn't see me in the same light I saw him. I was Max's little sister and nothing more.

And when I thought he had finally changed his mind, nine months ago, he crushed my heart.

Not on purpose. I know that now. Still, the pain was real. And I held onto that pain this entire year. Thinking he didn't want anything to do with me. That I was nothing more to him than a quick fuck. A one-night stand.

Wham bam thank you, ma'am!

I couldn't have been more wrong.

TWENTY-THREE

FINN

I SMELL HER BEFORE I SEE HER, A SMILE LIGHTING UP MY face I'm unable to hide. Thankfully, my back is to Max when he notices Willow.

"Hey!" I hear him say as he drops something heavy on the floor, close enough that I feel the thump beneath my shoes. "I'm so glad you're here."

Turning, I watch as he embraces his sister while my little tree stares at me over his shoulder, her eyes slowly taking me in from head to toe and back again. When they reach mine, I can see the fire blazing in them

"You said you needed a woman's opinion so here I am. How can I help?" Stepping out of Max's arms, she averts her eyes but not before shooting me a wink that sends a shot of adrenaline straight to my dick.

Why did I think this would be a good idea again?

Nothing good will come from painting with a hard-on.

It should have been done last week but we had to rip the carpet out first. That was a challenge in and of itself. Beneath the stains were old hardwood floors Max wanted to try and buff back to life. We spent two days trying to refinish them before giving up. They looked worse than when we started. There was too much damage.

"First, what do you think of the color?"

Motioning around the room, his arms spread, Max is smiling from ear to ear. When he catches sight of me, as if remembering I'm still here, his smile falls.

What the hell was that?

"Hey, Willow," I say, attempting to act casual.

"Finn," she states, her voice lacking emotion just like mine. "I like it, Maxy. The gray is soothing ... not too light, not too dark."

"That's what I was going for. Tensions tend to run high when we're in here. Meetings can get out of control quick. I'm hoping this makes for a calmer environment."

"Anything is better than the navy blue that was on the walls before," LT notes, glancing around to take in all the improvements we've done to the space. "Show me what else you two have been up to around here."

Leading her out of the room, I can hear Max listing all the things we've checked off his to-do list, his voice growing quieter as they ascend the stairs leading back up to the main level of the house. Adjusting myself in my pants to alleviate the strain on the zipper of my jeans, I dip the paint roller in the tray, soaking it, and returning my focus to the wall in front of me.

It's the last wall, thank God. I feel like I've spent most of my time in this one room the last nine days. I'm ready to clean up and lock the door behind me.

Colton and Kane are out picking up the new furniture in Colton's van. When they get back, we'll unload it into the den and that room will be finished as well. After that,

Max's list will be complete for the most part. Little things here and there, things he doesn't need me for.

After applying the final coat of paint, I stand back to admire my work and check to make sure the coverage is even. The lighting in here is shit, so I'm hoping the second coat will make it look better than it did when I started this morning.

"Looks good." Her voice is like music to my ears. I might see her every night—dream about her even when she's in my arms—but that doesn't mean I don't crave her presence. And I've been craving her more today than most since I didn't get to see her last night.

"Thanks," I say, glancing over my shoulder to see her leaning against the door frame. "So do you."

"Careful, hot shot. Max is on his way back down any second. Colt called, something about a table, and Max sounded angry. I walked away to give him some privacy."

"They're picking up furniture. I told them to rent a truck, but he insisted they could fit everything in his van. I'm assuming he was wrong."

"You assume correct," Max says, stepping past Willow, a look of frustration on his face. "Can you call Declan and see if he can go meet them?"

Nodding, I put the roller down, wipe my hands, and pull my phone out of my pocket. To my surprise, I have a text message waiting for me.

LT: You got a little paint on your ass. You should take your jeans off.

A fire blazes inside of me as I quickly shoot off a text

to Declan. He responds right away, asking for an address. Max rattles off the name of the store and where it's located. Once I've sent the information to my brother, I quickly reply to LT's message, so it doesn't look suspicious that I'm still typing.

ME: You first.

I hear her phone buzz in her purse, but she doesn't reach for it right away. Smart girl. Max is talking to her about the Memorial Day party, causing my ears to perk up. It's going to be a hell of a party. One I'm sure no one will forget. At least I know I won't. I just hope Max doesn't try and drown me in the pool.

Last night that's what I dreamt. He was holding me under water, laughing manically. I could see Willow standing by the edge of the pool, tears streaming down her face. And next to her, my brother holding Kendall's hand. They all watched but no one tried to stop Max.

That was the scariest part.

"Finn!" Max hollers.

Shaking the vision away, I look in Max's direction to find him glaring at me.

"Yeah, sorry. I'm fucking exhausted," I state, stretching my arms over my head to emphasize my point. It's not a lie. I didn't get much sleep before I woke up at four this morning gasping for breath. Needless to say, I wasn't able to fall back asleep.

"Whatever, man. I asked if you needed help cleaning this up?"

"I got it. What are you two up to?"

"Lo wants to take me shopping," he groans.

"You act like I'm going to girlify this place or something," she laughs. "I said you needed to put pictures on the wall, not that you needed pink throw pillows. A little art will class up the place. Manly stuff, I promise."

Rolling his eyes, Max wraps his arm over her shoulder and steers her toward the door. "Pray for me."

His parting words make me laugh along with Willow. I can't even be mad that I didn't get any alone time with her or that the closest we stood only allowed me to smell her perfume but not touch her.

Though, I do want to remedy that situation.

With my phone still in my hand, I shoot her one more text message before cleaning up all the paint supplies and washing the roller and brushes in the utility sink in the laundry room.

ME: Your place. Ten o'clock. Be naked.
LT: Make it eight and you have a deal. I'll cancel Taco Tuesday.

Sounds like my girl missed me as much as I missed her. I can't wait for all this sneaking around to be over. I could join her for Taco Tuesday. Pull her into my arms and kiss her whenever I want. It's all I can think about. Other than Max drowning me.

TWENTY-FOUR

WILLOW

POPPING THE HANDLE OF MY SUITCASE OUT, I ROLL IT OUT of my room and down the hall, hollering to Kendall as I pass her room, "Leaving in ten. Are you almost ready?"

"I have nothing to wear!" she whines. "I need to go shopping."

"It's not a fancy party. Bring a bathing suit and a sundress to wear over it. Sandals. What else do you need?" I ask, parking my suitcase by the front door and backtracking to her room.

I'm not prepared for the sight that greets me when I cross the threshold. Kendall's bed is covered in clothing. From dresses and skirts to tanks and tees. Her suitcase, however, lays empty on the floor next to the mess.

"Seriously?" I ask, scanning the room until my eyes stop on her.

She's standing in her closet. Most of the hangers are bare, clothes are piled around her feet, and she's scanning the little bit she has left still hanging.

This is not normal behavior for Kendall. If anything, she's the one usually helping me find an outfit to wear, waiting on me to finish getting ready before we leave. She loves to dress me up, in her clothes or mine, and create outfits I never would have put together myself. To say her wardrobe is vast is an understatement.

"Kendall, what's really going on?" I ask, stepping up behind her and placing my hand on her shoulder. When she turns to face me, I'm surprised to find her face stained with the remnants of tears. Without giving it a second thought, I pull her in and wrap my arms around her. "Talk to me," I beg.

"I have nothing to wear," she repeats, her words muffled against my shoulder.

"We both know that's a lie."

"I want to go shopping."

"Fine. We can go after we drop our bags at my mom's house. There's a cute little shop in the strip mall next to our subdivision. We'll make an afternoon out of it. I'll even see if Evie wants to come with us."

If there's one person Kendall likes to dress up more than me, it's my little sister. It's something she missed out on growing up. Kendall's twin, Kora, is a bit of a pill sometimes. One minute older, she acts superior. They were separated in school, Kora starting at five while they made Kendall wait to start the following year.

Everything between them is a competition and Kora is keeping score. From the time she was old enough to know what the phrase meant she's been keeping track. Kora crawled first, walked first. Had a boyfriend before Kendall and lost her virginity first. She graduated high school and will graduate college before K.

She's not a free spirit like Kendall and has always

treated her as a little sister instead of her equal. It's going to be nice not having her around this summer. She's off experiencing life, flying around the world as a flight attendant.

With K being treated as a little sister all her life, though, she never experienced what it was like to have one. So, when Evie is around, Kendall perks up and pretends Evie is her sister. She likes to dress her up and do the kinds of things she would for her own sister, if she let her.

"I guess we could do that," Kendall finally says, stepping back and looking around her room. Some of the hurricane of clothes she threw from her closet are going to have to come with us. Starting with a bathing suit just in case the little boutique doesn't sell any. The store is new, and I have yet to check it out.

"Let's grab a few of your favorites, get you packed, and then we'll go on a shopping spree to cheer you up. I'm sure Evie will be thrilled."

Nodding, Kendall numbly walks over and begins sifting through the piles, tossing clothing toward her open suitcase, not bothering to fold anything. Ten minutes later, she's fully packed and we're loading our suitcases into my VW Beetle.

I've spent the entire week on edge, nervous about tomorrow. The big reveal, as Kendall's been calling it.

Laugh it up, bitch. I'll remember this when you fall in love.

We're headed to my mom's house. Everyone else is coming tomorrow, including Finn and Max. Kendall and I promised to help my mom get the food ready for my parents' annual Memorial Day pool party. It's going to be hard to celebrate without Dad, but I know this is something Mom needs to do. We told her she could cancel it, but she refused.

The holidays were always a big deal with my parents. It didn't matter which holiday it was, or what we were celebrating. Birthdays, America's independence, Halloween ... they all required a party. As we got older and went off to college, Max and I took over some of the parties, especially the ones where we were at school and couldn't get away in the middle of the week. But things like Memorial Day, where they could host, they always have. And this year, even though Dad's not here and the pain is still raw, my mom insisted we keep with tradition.

"It's what he would have wanted."

She's right. Doesn't mean it's not going to be hard watching Max man the grill alone. That I'm not going to miss my dad laughing with his friends. Or that I'm not scared shitless that Max is going to blow a gasket tomorrow, even though he's not known for his public outbursts. This might just send him over the edge, and Dad won't be there to reel him back in.

"Finally," Evie says as soon as the screen door slams behind us. "I need to get out of here."

On the outside, my little sister looks perfect. She's a direct reflection of me in so many ways. The same height as me, a measly five foot three inches, a few pounds lighter, with eyes the exact same shade of blue. But outside appearances can be deceiving because the fire in those eyes is raging right now.

"Kendall wants to go shopping. Why don't you two

get out of here?" I suggest, knowing the bonding time will be good for both of them.

"Yes, please," Evie says at the same time Kendall chimes in with, "Sounds like a plan to me."

After snagging her car keys from the dish on the table, Evie and Kendall disappear out the front door without so much as a wave. I watch them go, Evie's hands flailing in the air as she bitches to Kendall about whatever has her on edge.

"She so much like you it's ridiculous sometimes. I can almost predict her next move," Mom says from behind me. When I turn, I find her drying her hands on a dish towel, her apron already around her waist. "Scrub in. We have food to make."

"What? No hello, how are you? No, I missed you?" I tease as I follow her into the kitchen and turn on the faucet.

"Hello, Lo. Nice to see you. I missed you so much. Now, are you ready to work? Because this is going to take all day with those two not helping."

"It's not that much. Last year you did it alone," I point out.

"No, last year I recruited Mary's help, but her and Chris are out of town until tomorrow."

Mary and Chris, Finn's parents, have been best friends with my parents for as long as I can remember. Because they were always around, so were Finn and his younger brothers, Declan, and Micah. We all got along, the boys acting like my brothers and all three of them protecting me and Evie like the sister they never had.

Declan even tried to convince Max to trade one of us

for Finn one year for Christmas. Said he would rather have a sister than an older brother who terrorized him. I volunteered Evie. Instead of trading his little sister for his best friend—something I was more than willing to do since I was ten and didn't realize what was really happening—Max threatened Declan's life. Something about cutting his hands off if he ever touched her. We all laughed, but I feel like the older we've gotten, the more serious Max's threats have become. It's probably a good thing Evie never showed any of those boys any interest.

"Will they be here?" I ask. Really, I want to ask if they'll be witness to the announcement Finn and I plan on making.

"Yeah. They're coming back tomorrow morning. It was a last-minute trip just to get away for the weekend."

I'm not sure whether to be relieved they'll be in attendance or upset. It means not having to go directly to them and make a statement. I love Chris and Mary. They've always been like second parents to me, and I don't want to do anything to make them look at me differently. Will they be happy about this?

"Happy about what?" my mother asks as I turn the faucet off. She hands me the towel she was using to dry my hands, holding onto it as she waits for me to answer her.

"What?" I realize I've said the words out loud but maybe she'll let it pass. Judging by the look of curiosity on her face the answer is no.

"What are you worried about telling the Grahams?"

"Uh," I start, not sure if Finn would be okay with me telling my mom without him here. It's not like I'm being given a choice, though. "So, you might want to sit down for a second."

Finally releasing the towel, my mother turns her body back toward the counter, picking up a knife. Her eyes finally leave mine as she begins dicing the onion on the cutting board in front of her.

"I'm good standing right here, Willow. What's going on?"

"Can you at least put down the knife?" I ask, not wanting her to cut herself.

"Talk," she demands.

So, I do. I tell her everything. From falling in love with Finn when I was only a teenager to our night last summer, leaving out details I know no mother wants to hear from her daughter, right up until the last few weeks. How he's helped me cope with the loss of Dad. That we've been sneaking around, lying to all our friends. Lying to Max. Mostly, how I've fallen head over heels in love with him.

The entire time I talk, my mother continues to chop her onion, moving on to dicing garlic, and finally cilantro. She nods her head in understanding from time to time, but her eyes never meet mine. And when I'm finished and she lays the knife down, I'm afraid of what I'll see when she finally faces me.

Tears.

Lots of tears.

If she were still chopping the onion, I'd assume they were from that. I can't seem to make it more than five seconds before the sting causes tears to well in my eyes most of the time. But that was at least fifteen minutes ago.

These tears are fresh, not from the pungent smell of an onion.

"Baby," she croaks out, opening her arms for me to wrap me in a hug. As soon as I step into her embrace, I relax. "I'm so happy for you. I always thought you two would end up together. So did your dad. He would be happy for you, you know that."

"You're only saying that because Dad knew Finn. I doubt *happy* is the word he would use right now. He'd say something sarcastic like, 'I need to give that boy another talking to,' or something."

"Of course he would, and that talk would be scary for Finn but that doesn't mean he doesn't love Finn. We've always seen the way you two love each other. From the time you were little. The first time you two were in the same room together it was like you migrated toward each other and it's been that way ever since."

Has it really? I don't remember the first time I met Finn, but I do feel the magnetic pull between us. I have for years.

"We're done keeping it a secret. We're planning on telling everyone tomorrow at the party. Figure it's our best chance at keeping Max from killing Finn."

"Don't worry about your brother," she says with confidence as she releases me from her hug. "He'll be fine, in time. It might take him a minute to get used to the idea, but I guarantee he's been mentally preparing for this for a long time. He's not blind, Willow. He's seen it, too, though the one time your dad tried to talk to him about it he denied it."

"Really?"

My mom laughs, a true carefree laugh, for the first time since my dad passed. It's like a knife straight to my heart. I've missed the sound of her laugh.

"Yeah, it went something like, 'Did you know Finn's in love with your sister?'" My mom imitating my father's voice has me holding back a giggle of my own. "And Max said something about killing Finn and locking you in your room until you were thirty."

"Wouldn't that be Dad's line?"

"You'd think, but your dad loved Finn. And he loved you. If Finn makes you happy that's all that would have mattered to him. Believe me, all he ever wanted was to make sure his kids were happy. Everything else was icing on the cake."

TWENTY-FIVE

FINN

THIRTY-SIX HOURS.

I realize it's not that long in the grand scheme of things. Still, not being able to hold LT last night, to feel her body curled against mine, her soft snoring assaulting my ears, was torture. Plain and simple.

Add to that the fact I had *another* nightmare about Max killing me and I'm ready for a nap even though it's only ten in the morning.

I have to hand it to my imagination, though. This time, my death was more creative. Instead of drowning me, Max tortured me first before slaying me with a light saber.

Star Wars was on in the background while we played poker with a few of the guys last night. It was Max's thank you for all our help this week, though really, I was the one who made out. Colton, Kane, and Julian were broke when they left, and Max had maybe two bucks in quarters, tapping out early.

My dream went a little something like this …

First there was the machete that appeared out of nowhere. He cut off my right hand for touching Willow.

Then Max pressed my face against the hot grill, making it so I couldn't open my left eye. You know, for looking at her.

The final, and most painful part of my dream was when he wielded a light saber and chopped off my dick.

No need to explain that move.

Again, all while people stood by and watched. Kendall and my brothers, one on either side of her, to Max's left. Tammy, Evie, and Willow standing off to his right. No one helped. No one hollered for him to stop.

I woke up in a cold sweat, immediately reaching for my cock to make sure it was still intact. I can't say for sure considering I was in a bit of a panic, but it may have been shriveled up slightly from the dream. Not that I would blame it. Hell, I was still shaking.

So, to be trapped in a car with Max for two hours feels like I'm headed to my death. My mind is consumed with all the possible ways he's going to react when we tell him. I texted LT this morning, making sure she was sure she wanted to do this, and our conversation didn't go as planned. I pissed her off on accident, made her doubt what we had.

ME: Morning. Miss you.
LT: Miss you more. What time are you guys leaving?
ME: About five minutes. We should be there a little after ten.
LT: Can't wait to see you. When do you want to tell everyone?
ME: Are you sure you want to do it today?

LT: Isn't that what you want? Or have you changed your mind?
ME: About us? No. There's no changing how I feel about you. About telling your brother …
LT: If this isn't what you want any more just say it, Finn.
ME: I want this, us, but I also want to live.
LT: He's not going to kill you. I promise. And I'll stop him if he even tries.

I contemplated telling her about the dreams. About how she stood by and watched him chop off my dick with a glowing blue beam, but I don't. It would take too long to explain, and I didn't want to relive the nightmare.

ME: I think I'm just worried about how he's going to react. This is what I want. Please don't doubt that.
LT: Good, because if it wasn't, I may have had to chop your dick off.

Her choice of words cause me to shiver. What is it with this family and chopping off my favorite body part?

ME: You are all I care about. You are all I want.
LT: Good answer. I'll see you in a few hours.

We talked about how we wanted to announce our relationship the other night. Instead of yelling that we're sleeping together—one, since it's already been done, and two, since we saw how Max reacted last time and we don't want a repeat—we're going to casually let people figure it out.

If they ask, we won't deny it. I'm allowed to hold her hand, put my arm around her, kiss her with our friends around. But before any of that can happen, we're going to pull Max aside and tell him the truth. It's the respectful thing to do.

To ensure he doesn't go ape shit on my ass, I asked LT if we could at least wait until the party started. I want there to be other people around, in the general area, so he keeps him temper in check. Otherwise, one of my dreams might become my reality. Since light sabers aren't a real thing, I'm guessing I'd be drowning in the pool.

Not how I want to go out.

I'm too young to die. I have too much to live for. Too many things I want to experience in life, with Willow by my side. Max too.

At the end of the day, no matter what happens, he will always be my best friend. Do I want his blessing? Absolutely. If I don't get it, will I back away? Not a chance in hell.

I'll just have to work harder to prove to him that I'm good enough to be with Willow.

"You okay over there?" Max asks, pushing against my shoulder.

"Yeah, man. Fine."

"Really? Because you don't seem fine. Your knee's been bouncing up and down the last ten miles. Your hands are clenched in your lap. And don't even get me started on how you've been staring at the glove compartment like it's somehow wronged you."

DIRTY LITTLE SECRET

"Just a little nervous I guess," I admit before I realize what I'm saying. "I know it's going to be weird for you today, and the girls. To be honest, it's going to be weird for me, too. I loved your dad and it's hard to imagine a Memorial Day party without him in front of the grill."

"Yeah," he sighs. "I'm glad my mom is doing this, but at the same time, it feels too soon. It's only been a little over a month and the wound is still fresh. Every time I go home it's like reopening it again."

That may be the most honest statement Max has shared with me in weeks. Especially where it concerns his dad.

"It'll get easier. It has to. We all deal differently and in our own time. Don't rush it but don't ignore it either. Let yourself feel, Max. It's the only way you will eventually be able to heal."

"You been talking to Lo?" he asks.

"Wh-What? Wh-Why?" My voice betrays me, stuttering.

"You sound just like her."

"Oh, no. Must be the psych class I took freshman year. I'm sure she took the same one."

The car falls silent as Max takes the exit for his parents' house. Fifteen minutes and we'll be pulling in their driveway. A few hours from now our friendship will be teetering on the edge of the abyss. I can only hope he accepts my love for his sister and that if he does try to drown me, someone jumps in to save me.

TWENTY-SIX

WILLOW

MY HANDS ARE SHAKING, THE BOWL OF POTATO SALAD I'M carrying feeling unsteady. Our house is full of family and friends, a multitude of conversations floating on the warm summer breeze. Kendall's been by my side most of the day, helping with the food and making sure the punch bowl never gets below half full.

Which is turning into a bad idea since she keeps adding more and more alcohol and not much else.

She's as fidgety as I am today. I've tried to get her to talk to me, more to distract me from my own nerves than anything else, but she refuses. Then she disappeared for thirty minutes earlier only to return a little less on edge, her hair a mess.

Well, if that didn't confirm my suspicions that she's secretly seeing one of our friends, nothing is going to.

I only wish I'd been paying closer attention to who else was missing from the party. The only people we're waiting on to arrive are Finn's parents. Then, Finn and I are going to pull Max aside.

I'm not ready.

After our text exchange this morning, I don't feel as confident as I did. Finn swears he's not second guessing our decision to go public, but I can't help but wonder what has him concerned. He's the one who's wanted to tell Max from the beginning. He's the one who was pressuring me to be honest with my brother.

And suddenly he's what … having a change of heart?

Not that I think he doesn't love me. I know he does. But something is obviously bothering him, and before we make our relationship official, I need to know what it is.

After dropping off the fresh bowl of potato salad on the buffet my mother and Evie set up this morning, I head in search of Finn for answers. He's talking with Declan in hushed tones, his face flushed with anger. When he catches my eye and I nod my head toward the pool house, he shoots me a sly wink.

Skirting the side of the small building, I head down to the tree and wait for him to join me. The last time I was down here was the day of my father's funeral. It was also the day our secret affair began. I knew there was no turning back the second our lips connected, and as scared as I am that he holds my heart, I also know we're right together.

He's my other half.

We are meant to be together.

Which means this conversation should be easy, but it feels like an elephant is sitting on my chest.

"Hey, beautiful," Finn says, taking a seat in the shade next to me.

"Hey yourself. I've barely seen you today. What's going on with Declan?"

Finn grunts in disapproval but doesn't answer my question. "What's going on with you? You looked like you needed to talk."

"I just ... I don't know. You're hesitating. It makes me wonder if this is really what you want? Not me but telling everyone. Telling Max."

Wrapping his arm around my shoulder, he pulls me close, and I rest my head in the crook of Finn's shoulder. He lets out a long sigh but doesn't reply right away. When he does, his confession shocks me.

"I love you, Willow. There is no doubt in my mind. My heart belongs to you. When you walk in the room it screams in triumph. *Mine!* But I won't lie to you. I'm scared as fuck to tell your brother."

"I love you, too," I whisper.

"You have no idea how happy it makes me to hear you say that. The dreams I've been having made me doubt telling Max."

"Dream?"

Finn tells me about the nightmares that have woken him up this past week. The anger he saw on Max's face. How we all stood by and watched as Max tried to kill him.

I'm holding back my laughter by the time he finishes telling me about the light saber incident, my body shaking in his arms.

"Not as funny as you think, LT. I was petrified when I woke up."

"Yes, but," I start, letting out a giggle, "you have to admit it's a little bit funny. I mean, come on. Max might be mad, he might not understand ... hell, he may not talk to either one of us for a while, but as far as violence goes, the worst that'll happen would be his fist landing on your face."

"That's what you think. He's always been protective of you and Evie. Since your dad passed, it's only intensified. I get it, I do. I don't have sisters, but if I did, I wouldn't want anyone touching them either. Still, I wish he could see how much I love you. That I'd do anything to protect you. That to me you're more than just a fling, you're my everything."

"And you're mine," I reply, lifting my head so our lips can meet.

"Do you really mean it?"

My body goes still at the sound of Max's voice. He's close enough that I know he can see my lips pressed against Finn's. His words tell me he heard our entire conversation.

Pulling away, Finn and I both turn our heads in Max's direction to find him standing only a few feet away. Arms crossed over his chest. Lips pinched in a firm line.

"I do." Finn's voice is strong, firm.

"How long?" Max asks. His voice is laced with anger and something else I can't put my finger on.

"I've loved her for years."

When Max looks in my direction, I echo Finn's words.

"How long have you been lying to me?" This time I can clearly identify what his voice has been trying to mask. Hurt, betrayal.

Yes, he's angry. I'm sure this isn't what he expected to find when he came down here. Or to hear for that matter. This isn't how we wanted to tell him. I had my speech all planned out.

Maxy, my favorite brother, I'd start. Buttering him up a bit before dropping the hammer. Then I'd take Finn's hand in mine. *I'm in love with your best friend and he's in love with me. We've been in love with each other for a long time and we don't want to hide it anymore. If you love me, you'll accept this.*

Those daydreams always ended with us hugging and Max accepting Finn as my boyfriend.

The nightmares weren't as pleasant. Nothing compared to the kinds of terror Finn has been dreaming about, but fists always flew, and Finn always walked away bloody and bruised.

We're about to find out if I'm living a daydream or a nightmare.

"Since Dad died," I offer before Finn can answer. "The funeral."

"You've been sneaking around for over a month? Lying to me and everyone else every day? Pretending nothing is going on when I'm around?" When neither of us reply, Max continues, a slow smirk spreading across his face as he does, shocking the hell out of me. "That's all?"

"What do you mean *that's all*?" I practically shout, pushing off the ground.

"You two have been in love with each other for years. I assumed you were sneaking around a lot longer than that. I'm surprised it took you this long to stop fighting your feelings."

I feel my mouth drop as I stare at my brother. He knew. This whole time, he knew we loved each other. He never said a word. Never tried to keep us apart.

When I feel Finn's arms snake around my waist, I let my body slump against his.

"Does this mean you're not going to try and drown me?" Finn asks from behind me.

I can't see his face, but I can hear the smile in his voice.

"Not today."

"You're not going to hit me?" Finn asks, needing confirmation that his life isn't in danger.

"Depends on if you fuck this up or not. Hurt her and I'll reconsider both options. You'll never even see me coming."

"If he hurts me, I'll drown him myself," I state, standing up a little taller, my head brushing against Finn's chin.

Damn him for being so tall. Though, I do fit perfectly against his body.

"I'd pay to see that." Max laughs, stepping forward and extending his fist to Finn. I watch in awe as they bump, a heavy sigh leaving me only after Max turns and walks back to the party.

"That went better than I thought it would," Finn says after Max disappears out of sight.

"Is that your way of saying you're happy you get to keep your dick?" I joke. His body stiffens against mine. "Kidding. Calm down. It was never in danger and we both know it."

"If you say so."

He squeezes me tight, and I let my body relax against Finn's again, enjoying the fact we no longer have to hide what we are. How much we care about each other. The lying and sneaking around is over. As hot as it was, I'm ready to openly be a part of his life.

"So, *girlfriend*, are you ready to go tell the rest of our friends that you couldn't keep your hands off me?"

"Right. Like they'd believe that."

"But that is how all this started. You, in my bed last summer. Running your hand over my chest. Practically begging me to touch you, to taste you." My knees shake at the memory of that night. For nine months I block it all out, wanting to forget every detail because it hurt too much. And now ... a replay is in order. "I wanted you for years but never thought I'd have you. Until that night. It changed everything."

Yes, yes it did.

And even with all the pain associated with it, I wouldn't change that night for the world.

"We should get back to the party before I strip you down and have my way with you right here. Your brother may be cool with us being together, but I can't imagine he'd appreciate a front row seat of you naked, riding my cock."

My body buzzes at the thought, knowing how easy it would be for him to lift up the skirt of my dress right now and slide into me.

"What if we skipped the get naked part? No one would ever know what we were doing ..." I let my voice trail off.

Finn's arms tighten their hold on me, pulling me against his body. His erection pokes my lower back, letting me know he's more than ready to make that fantasy a reality.

"Have a seat, Mr. Graham," I state, pulling out of his embrace and motioning to the grass beneath the tree where we'll be blocked from view of anyone coming over the hill from the party.

With a sense of urgency, Finn lowers himself to the ground, pops the button on his jeans, and releases his swollen cock. Holding himself by the base, he slowly pumps, the head turning purple.

He's ready for me, there's no doubt in my mind.

"Condom?" I ask, moving to stand with one foot on either side of his thighs.

"Fuck," he swears under his breath. "I don't have my wallet. I left it in your brother's car."

"You mean you weren't planning on having your way with me at some point today?" I joke as he runs one hand up my thigh, under my dress, to the place I want him to touch me the most. All while continuing to pump his engorged cock.

"It's all I've been thinking about. All last night. On the ride here. Then I saw you in this dress and I had to look away, so I didn't have a tent in my pants." When he reaches the apex of my thighs, brushing over my sensitive nub, I throw my head back and let out a moan.

"I want you inside of me, Finn," I say as he continues to touch me, my underwear becoming an unwelcome barrier.

"I know, baby. I know. For now, though, this is all we can do. Sit down on me and I'll take care of you."

Lowering myself to sit straddling his thighs, I grind down on his cock, causing both of us to suck in a breath.

"Fuck, Willow."

"I can't wait. I don't want to. You're all I want. The only man I've ever wanted, Finn. Please," I beg. "Don't make me wait."

"This isn't a good idea, you know. It's playing with fire," he says through clenched teeth as I grind against him again, the tip of his cock pressing the thin fabric of my panties inside of me.

"I'm on the pill, remember," I try to rationalize with him. We had that conversation after our first night together when he completely forgot to wrap himself before sliding into me.

"That's not it. I want you, with nothing between us. Always. No more condoms. But I also don't want to screw this up and get you pregnant before you're ready. Before we're ready." We're both panting, the friction almost too much to bear. I'm dangerously close to the edge. One more push and I'll be free falling into nothing. "I want us to do this right. I want to marry you first."

And that's all it takes.

Lightning shoots from my toes straight to my core and then the rest of my body. My head falls against Finn's chest as he begins thrusting upward, his cock rubbing against my clit, helping me ride out my orgasm as he finds his own release, pulling back and coming all over the inside of my thigh.

"I love you," he says through strangled breaths.

I press my lips to the side of his neck. "I love you more."

TWENTY-SEVEN

Finn

Willow's laughter catches the attention of a few of our friends as we approach, hand in hand. I'm trying to convince her to let me yell that we're sleeping together, the way I did only weeks ago to get Max and Evie to stop talking, but she refuses. Apparently, I need to work on my negotiation skills with her.

Promises of sexual favors didn't work.

She's never been one to swoon over flowers, but her love of Twix and most other chocolate candy bars I thought would at least have her considering letting me announce our relationship with flair.

Nope.

She's not budging.

Her reasoning?

If Max suspected something, if he saw our love even though we weren't together, so did everyone else. There's no reason to make a big fuss over it. She wants to let it be what it is.

We don't need to announce it because it's not going to make a damn bit of difference in our circle.

I have to admit, my girl is right, but that doesn't mean I don't want to claim her in front of everyone.

"Finally coming out of the closet?" I hear Kendall whisper to LT as we slide up next to her and Evie.

"Yeah. You should try it," I say, catching her eye. Kendall's stare hardens but she doesn't stomp off like I expect her to. Probably because my brother is only a few feet away, listening to our conversation.

I saw them sneak away earlier. They were sly enough no one else caught on but their secret is going to be exposed eventually.

"I'd like to propose a toast," Max announces, standing on one of the loungers around the pool. Everyone turns to give him their full attention. "To great friends and family. Thank you for being here today. This is exactly what my dad would have wanted, and even though he's not here, I imagine he's smiling down on us today. Also, to my best friend and my sister, Lo. It's about damn time they figured their shit out."

"Maxwell," Tammy scolds.

"Sorry, Mom," he mumbles, but keeps his glass held high as he continues. "To two people who mean the world to me and to each other," he states, gazing in our directions. "May she give you hell for as long as you let her."

Our friends and family laugh, raising their glasses in the air and shouting, "Cheers."

"And you thought you were getting out of an announcement," I whisper against LT's ear before tugging it with my teeth. When I pull back to stare into her eyes, I find them rolling at my comment. "What?"

"I said it was inappropriate for you to yell we were having sex."

"First comes love." I kiss her forehead. "Then comes marriage." I kiss her cheek. "Then comes little Finns in a baby carriage."

Pressing my lips to her, I silence her protests. When she pushes against my chest, I release her, unable to contain my laugh at the expression on her face.

"You think you're hilarious, don't you?" I can tell she's trying to hold back her own laugh. Her lips are pressed together in a smile.

She's happy.

She's mine.

Which means I'm happy.

I don't care who knows it.

"I have my moments. You can't say I'm wrong."

"I don't see a ring on my finger," she challenges. When I open my mouth, she places her hand over it. "Don't go getting any ideas, Finn. It was a joke."

"Whatever you say." My words are muffled by her fingers, but I know she heard me, rolling her eyes again.

"Can you two stop eye-fucking each other for five seconds," Kendall growls, her voice filled with irritation.

"Sorry. This is what I signed up for, and I plan on taking advantage of it every second of every day." My eyes bore into LT's as I say the words, Kendall's reply barely registering as she storms off.

"Be nice. She's having a rough day. Piper and Alexis can't make it out today, and I can tell she's lonely."

"Not from what I saw earlier. She disappeared with—"

"No!" Willow screams, catching the attention of both my brothers and Max who are only a few feet away. "I don't want to know."

Now I'm rolling my eyes. "Fine, but I hope you realize that whatever is going on between them, it's only just starting. If you want to be there for your friend, you need to know whose roller coaster she's riding."

"That was a really bad pun." Groaning as she closes her eyes, LT's body shivers. "I can't unsee what I saw."

Yeah, neither can I.

"Want to get out of here?"

I want to be alone with my girl. To hold her in my arms.

"We can't. The party has barely started. Your parents just got here. We haven't even said hi to them yet."

Nodding in understanding, I take her hand in mine and let her lead me around the yard. Our friends congratulate us, some pretending to be shocked while others sport a knowing grin. The only people I think we truly shocked today are my parents. I know Willow's parents always suspected there was something between us but mine seemed to have been oblivious.

With the slight nod of his head, my father pulls me aside, away from Willow who's engrossed in conversation with my mother.

"What's up?"

"I'm happy for you, son. James would be, too."

I really fucking hope so. His blessing would mean a lot to me.

"Thanks, Dad."

"Have you really loved her forever?" He seems

surprised. When my mother asked for the details of how we fell in love, Willow simply said it started a long time ago.

"For as long as I can remember," I answer honestly.

He only nods before changing the subject. "What's going on with your brother? I saw you two arguing earlier. That doesn't happen every day."

No, it doesn't. In fact, I can't remember the last time I fought with either of them to the point I had to hold back from physically harming them.

"He's being an ass, screwing around with a girl. I warned him off a little while ago, but he didn't listen. She's one of Willow's friends, so I was a little hot when I found out he didn't end it."

"What if there's more to it than you know? I mean, look at you and Willow. Sometimes there's more than meets the eye."

He has a good point, but knowing my brother, there's no way he feels the same way about Kendall that I do about Willow. We've known each other for years. I'm not even sure when their tryst got started. Maybe that's what I should have asked him instead of yelling about fucking her in the Palmers' bathroom.

Which he claims he didn't do.

His exact words were, "No penetration," like that makes whatever went on in there better.

"You're right." Nodding at my father, I look around in search of Declan. He's still standing with Micah and Max, but his eyes are focused on Kendall across the pool. And hers? They're locked on his.

Fuck. Shit's about to get complicated.

The way they're looking at each other confirms they're more than just a fling. Because I know that look in his eyes. I've seen it in my own reflection. He's a possessed man.

TWENTY-EIGHT

Finn

Max has been unusually quiet the entire ride back to town. I was going to catch a ride with LT, but Max insisted I ride with him. After the way he reacted to finding out about our relationship, I didn't give it a second thought.

He's okay with this.

Happy even, it seems.

Why would I worry about being alone in a car with him for two hours?

The silence, that's why.

I can tell there's a storm brewing. His hands are clenched around the steering wheel. His breathing is deep and slow, as if he's trying his best to keep himself calm. The closer we get to our loft, the more I start to get nervous about whatever is on his mind. And I keep circling back to me being with Willow. Without asking him for permission even though he made it sound like we'd had it all along.

We still live together.

He's still my best friend.

If he's not okay with me dating Willow, I want to talk it out. Hell, I'll break out the boxing gloves and we can go a few rounds. Nothing is going to change my mind about being with her, though. I love her. Someday I plan to marry her. And when that day comes, since James is gone, I'll ask Max for his blessing.

Chancing a glance in his direction, I watch as his hands twist against the leather of the steering wheel.

No time like the present to clear the air. At least he can't hit me right now.

"What's on your mind, Max? I can see there's something."

Please don't let it be me and Willow.

"Just thinking." His words are clipped, his anger evident.

"Anything you want to share?" My gut says to let it go, but I know the more Max let's something simmer, the angrier he'll be when he finally let's go. If it's the difference between dealing with an EF-0 tornado and an EF-5, I'll take the zero any day. Lower chance of any casualties.

He seems to contemplate my offer before speaking. "How long have you really loved her?"

"Years," I say without hesitation.

"You know, last summer, I tried to push you two together."

Say what?

"I saw there was something there. Neither one of you could keep your eyes off the other. So that last party we had before school started, I thought, why not? Let's see if this is the real deal or if they just need to get it out of their system. Not that I wanted you to fuck my sister and never talk to her again," he clarifies. "And then the next morning, she was gone. I was so pissed. The way I saw it, you used her. You got what you wanted, and she did the walk of shame the next morning. Did I know for sure you slept together? No, but your face was laced with guilt."

"It's not what you think," I try to explain, but he only shakes his head.

"I don't want to know what happened. All I need to hear is that you two aren't just a fling. That you're going to take care of my sister, treat her right."

"Of course I will, man. I'd never do anything to hurt her." I hope he can hear the sincerity in my words. No matter what my relationship with Willow has been over the years—friends or lovers—I've always treated her with love.

"I know I said I was okay with this, but the more I think about it, the angrier I get," he confesses.

No shit. Anger has been radiating off him in waves the last ninety minutes.

"Listen, I get that I might not be the man you'd pick for Willow—"

"That's just it. You are. Since we were kids. You were the one I always thought would break our pact. The one I figured would take her virginity. I was convinced I was going to have to kill you for touching her. But you never did. Then I tried to push you together and that didn't work out. Maybe I'm just pissed that it wasn't on my terms. Or maybe I'm mad you kept it from me. I don't know. I'm happy for you guys, but I'm also irate at the same time. Does that even make sense?"

He wanted us together. He would have picked me for her.

"Why?" It's all I can focus on right now. "Why me? Why would you have let me date Willow but not the other guys?"

"You're my best friend, Finn. If there's anyone in this world I can trust to take care of her, it's you. The fact you stayed away from her when you clearly didn't want to, because of a pact we made a long ass time ago, speaks volumes about your character. You're a loyal friend and you'll be loyal to Willow. And if I'm wrong, I'll just kill you."

My best friend is threatening me. I mean, it is his sister we're talking about, but you'd think there would have been at least a hint of humor in his voice.

Nope.

It was flat. I can tell he's serious as hell.

Not that I plan on hurting Willow. Never in a million years do I want that to happen but I'm not perfect. We're going to fight from time to time. She's strong and opinionated, and as laid back as I can be, I'm not as go-with-the-flow as people tend to think I am. Butting heads is inevitable but I'm looking forward to it.

The make-up sex will be fantastic.

"Noted," I state, keeping my voice as firm as his. "We cool then? Because you're wearing out the leather on your steering wheel."

Max glances down at his hands. His death grip has caused his knuckles to turn white. As soon as he loosens his grip, they pink back up, causing Max to chuckle to himself.

"We're cool. As long as I don't hear about you two having sex. Or actually hear you in the act. I might not be able to hold back from punching you in the face. She's still my little sister."

I can't help but laugh as Max's face scrunches up in a grimace.

Mental note to self: no loud sex when Max is home.

"Thanks, man," I say as he hits his blinker for our exit.

"For what?" You can hear the confusion in his voice as he glances over at me.

"Trusting me with her. Not hitting me when we told you. I promise not to let you down."

"Damn straight you won't. You break her heart, I break your face," he threatens, this time with a smile.

"Breaking my face would be mild in comparison to what I dreamed you might do to me," I start, launching into details about the dreams I had. I don't think I've ever heard Max laugh so loud in his life. His face is bright red, and he's gasping for breath by the time we reached our loft.

He's a damn good brother and friend. One day I'm hoping to call him both.

TWENTY-NINE

WILLOW

I HEAR THE FRONT DOOR TO MY APARTMENT OPEN AND then the soft click of the lock sliding into place. He's early. I wasn't expecting him for another ten minutes or so. We were going to stay at his place tonight, but Max invited the guys over for poker. Finn said he was going to play a few hands and then come over. He promised not to make me wait that long, but if he's walking in right now, he basically followed me out. Not very subtle. It's only been a few weeks since we've started seeing each other publicly and we're still trying to find our balance.

It's awkward for me to stay at his place, knowing Max is there. That he might hear something. The first night I did, coffee the next morning was tense. I know he's okay with our relationship but that doesn't mean he wants to see me with crazy sex hair or watch as a half-naked Finn kisses me.

So, we stay here most nights. Poor Kendall is probably sick of us invading her space. And tonight, I feel bad because we weren't supposed to be here. She was already asleep when I snuck in an hour ago, probably catching up after the look of exhaustion I saw on her face this morning. She's been working herself to the bone between summer camp and the daycare center. She loves kids, but being around them all day, every day has to be physically and mentally draining.

Footsteps sounds in the hall, so I slip my robe off my shoulders, toss it in the corner, and open my bedroom door. Finn thought I was mad at him for changing our plans tonight, so I want to show him I'm not harboring any ill feelings about his poker game. I want us to have our separate lives, to be able to do our own thing, but also spend time together. With and without our friends around.

Tonight, without is preferred.

The hallway is dark, but I watch as he approaches, his footsteps faltering when he notices me standing in the doorway, naked. My back is arched against the doorframe, my chest pushed out. He's seen all of me but that doesn't mean I'm not somewhat self-conscious, so I cross my legs to hide his second favorite part of my body from the naked eye.

Get it … naked eye! Ha!

Oh, by the way, his favorite part of my body is my heart. At least that's what he tells me. I'm inclined to believe him since he owns it. It beats for him and only him.

"It's about time," I coo, keeping my voice low so I don't wake Kendall.

"Willow?"

Holy shit! That's not Finn's voice.

Jumping back inside of my room, I slam my door. My heart's pounding against my chest as I attempt to wrap my brain around what just happened. There's a knock at my door, startling me.

"Can we talk?" he asks.

I can hear the strain in his voice. I guarantee he wasn't expecting what he saw either.

"Um, just a second," I holler, scrambling across the room to find my robe. Once it's secured around my waist, I crack my door open and stare into the darkness.

He's close enough I can see the outline of his five o'clock shadow. Just like his brother's.

"What are you doing here, Declan?" I ask as Kendall's door whips open.

Realization dawns on me.

Declan and Kendall. He was the mystery man on the couch. And the reason Finn was so upset about it. Everything is starting to make sense now. Why he was so opposed to them being together.

"Can we not tell Finn what just happened?" he asks instead of answering me.

"Um, he's on his way over here right now."

"Fuck," he mutters, scrubbing his hands down his face. A classic Graham brothers move. "Can we leave out the part where I saw you naked? Please," he begs.

I'm shaking my head before he finishes, and Declan lets out a sigh. "Of course not. You two are always honest with each other, aren't you?"

"Better to be honest and hurt yourself than to lie and hurt someone else."

Before he can reply again, Kendall comes storming out into the hall. The next few minutes are a flurry of activity. Declan apologizing. Kendall yelling at him about being here, freaking out. Finn knocking on the door. Declan getting into an argument with Finn. Kendall crying and storming off to her room.

And me?

I stand there and say nothing. I let the events unfold in front of me, numb to it all.

Kendall refuses to open her door for Declan, who eventually gives up and leaves at Finn's urging. After he's gone, Finn drags me back to my room, muttering something about us staying at his place from now on. I can feel the anger radiating off him in waves.

That's when I snap out of my trance.

"I need to talk to Kendall," I state.

"You might want to give her a second to cool off. She was pretty upset."

"Because you called Declan a man-whore in front of her. You made her feel used." My words hold no malice. I know that's not what he was trying to do. He was angry with Declan, and Kendall was an unfortunate victim of his poor choice of words.

"Shit," he growls, running his fingers through his already tousled hair. "I should probably apologize to her."

"Let me talk to her first. I'll be back in a minute."

After lightly knocking on her door, I tighten the belt on my robe as I wait for Kendall it.

"Come in," she calls, her voice hoarse.

She's sitting with her legs crossed in the middle of her bed. I close the door behind me, take a seat next to her, and wrap my arms around her, resting my chin on her shoulder.

"I thought you were staying at Finn's place tonight," she starts.

"Poker game. Change of plans. I would have told you, but I thought you were asleep." She doesn't say anything, so I continue, "You don't have to change your life to accommodate me, K. You live here, too. You can have over whoever you want whenever you want. You know that."

"I didn't invite him over. He just showed up."

"The Graham boys are persistent, aren't they?" I try to keep my voice light and playful, but her face remains stoic.

"No one was supposed to know anything. Not that there's much to tell."

"I'm sorry," I say, meaning every word of it. "You could have told me, ya know? I would have understood. Those boys have a magnetism about them that's hard to deny."

"You can say that again," she mutters into my shoulder.

"I can tell you really like him."

"I don't know anymore."

"No more lies, K. Dec's a good guy."

"According to your boyfriend, his brother, he's a man-whore. What does that make me?" she asks, her voice choking up.

"He's not a man-whore, for starters. Finn's just angry. He warned Declan to stay away from you if he wasn't serious about you, so when he found him here in the middle of the night ... well, it was clear Dec wasn't listening to him."

"It's not Finn's job to protect me."

"Try telling him that," I joke. "You matter to me, so you matter to him. He'll protect you with all he has, even from his own brother."

Kendall doesn't say anything. There's no reason to argue with me. We both know Finn would go to war with Declan if necessary.

"I think I just need to let him go," she finally whispers, more to herself than to me.

"If that's what you want."

"I don't know what I want anymore. One minute it's him, the next it's anyone but him."

"That's what you need to figure out then. Decide what you want. What makes you happy."

We sit in silence for a few minutes before Kendall kicks me out so she can go to sleep. I contemplate staying with her, holding her the way I know I'd want to be held if the situation were reversed, but Kendall's not me.

If she wanted me here, she'd ask me to stay. She wants to be alone, to think, and because I respect her, I leave her to do just that.

"She okay?" Finn asks as I slide under the covers. He tucks me against his chest, wrapping his arms around me as I get comfortable.

"She will be. She just needs to figure out what she wants. I know she really likes your brother but she's also afraid. I think her feelings are what scare her the most."

"I'll kick his ass if he breaks her heart."

"No, you won't. Because that's not what Kendall would want. She can fight her own battles. If he hurts her, she'll hurt him back. It'll be ugly." Which is what worries me. Because I love Declan like a brother and Kendall like a sister. A war between them would be like a war in the family.

"I feel like I should have told you it was Dec even though you didn't want to know," Finn confesses, kissing the top of my head.

"It wouldn't have made any difference. Kendall wasn't ready to talk about it. She still isn't. She's confused. If I hadn't caught him sneaking in tonight, I still wouldn't know who he was."

"Maybe I should talk to my brother. My dad said something that had me thinking maybe this was more than just a fling, but how he reacted earlier ... I need to find out what really happened tonight."

"About that ..." I start, letting my voice trail off as I turn in his arms so I'm facing him. "The hall was dark, and I may have thought Declan was you when he walked in."

"I'm not surprised. Same height, same build."

He's not going to like what I have to say next, so before I speak, I place my hand over his heart. "And I wasn't expecting anyone else to be sneaking in our apartment."

"Willow," he says, his voice filled with warning.

"And I may have been standing in the doorway waiting for you." He growls, not liking where this is headed, but I can't not tell him, so I spill the last tidbit of information. "Naked."

"What?" he yells.

"Shhh. Kendall is trying to sleep. I'm not even sure she knows what happened."

"My brother saw you naked?" he asks, not bothering to lower his voice.

"It was dark. I could barely see him, so I'm not sure how much he saw. Maybe a boob," I try to joke, but the thunderous expression on Finn's face tells me he doesn't find me or the situation the least bit funny.

"I'm going to have to kill him now." He makes the statement sound so simple. Like a decision has already been made.

"No, you don't. Plus, it's not like I let him touch me. All of this," I say, scooting away from him and running my hands down the front of my body, "belongs to you and only you. Always you."

Finn let's out a possessive growl as he flips me on my back and hovers over me.

"Mine." Aggression and love combine to make the single word take on a whole new meaning.

"Yours," I agree, smiling up at him. "What are you gonna do with it is my question?"

"I think you know exactly what I'm going to do, my little tree."

His voice is filled with promise, his words soft and sweet as he makes love to me. Showing me with his body everything I already know.

I belong to him, and he belongs to me.

Heart. Body. Soul.

Stay tuned for Kendall's story in Tempting Little Tease!

ABOUT THE AUTHOR

Rachael Brownell is an award-winning author of young-adult and new-adult romance. She resides in the midwest with her husband and son. To learn more about Rachael and her books, follow her on social media or join her reader group on Facebook, Brownell's Book Lovers.

For more information…
www.AuthorRachaelBrownell.com
rachael@authorrachaelbrownell.com

ALSO BY RACHAEL BROWNELL

Friends-to-lovers Romance…

A Moment Too Late

For All The Wrong Reasons

For All The Right Reasons

Worth The Fight

Chasing Fate

Second-chance Romance…

Half Truths

Always in My Heart

A Million Little Reasons

Imperfect Love Story

Imperfect Love Story: New Beginnings

Sticks & Stones

The Love or Lust Series

Dark, gritty, sexy Romance…

Caught in the Storm

Surviving the Storm

Office Romance…

Damaging Rumors

Devious Rumors

Delicate Rumors

Deserving Rumors

Devastating Rumors

Defensive Rumors

Young-adult Romance...

Holding On

Unglued

Weakness

Flawed Reality

Take A Gamble

Snapshot